"Kyle, this i
Amber said

"We have nothing to quarrel about," she continued. "You kissed me and I liked it. I'd like you to do it again. There's nothing wrong with that, and you're leaving the day after tomorrow. Why can't we be friends?"

"Friends?" Kyle shook his head. "I hoped for that, too, at first. But tonight has brought home to me that I want more than friendship from you, Amber."

"What more?" Amber asked doubtfully. "You don't want love. You said so."

Kyle sighed, "Use your imagination, kitten." His voice was very dry.

"Oh," said Amber, as the light dawned. "Oh, I see. You want my—my . . ."

"I want your beautiful body, Amber, darling," Kyle finished bleakly. "And as I have no intention of taking it, I'd find it very hard to be 'just friends.'"

Kay Gregory grew up in England but moved to Canada as a teenager. She now lives in Vancouver with her husband, two sons, one dog and two ferrets. She has had innumerable jobs, some interesting, some extremely boring, which have often provided background for her books. Now that she is writing Harlequin romance novels, Kay thinks she has at last found a job that she won't find necessary to change.

Books by Kay Gregory

HARLEQUIN ROMANCE
2919—A STAR FOR A RING
3016—A PERFECT BEAST
3058—IMPULSIVE BUTTERFLY

Don't miss any of our special offers. Write to us at the following address for information on our newest releases.

Harlequin Reader Service
901 Fuhrmann Blvd., P.O. Box 1397, Buffalo, NY 14240
Canadian address: P.O. Box 603,
Fort Erie, Ont. L2A 5X3

AMBER
AND AMETHYST
Kay Gregory

Harlequin Books

TORONTO • NEW YORK • LONDON
AMSTERDAM • PARIS • SYDNEY • HAMBURG
STOCKHOLM • ATHENS • TOKYO • MILAN

Original hardcover edition published in 1990
by Mills & Boon Limited

ISBN 0-373-03082-7

Harlequin Romance first edition October 1990

THIS BOOK IS DEDICATED TO
My friend and fellow novelist
CAROLINE JANTZ
With thanks for all her
support, help, information and dedication
to the world of Romance

CHAPTER ONE

SHE must be seeing things.

Amber's grey-green eyes had been drooping from sheer boredom, but suddenly they snapped open and she sat up very straight. Surely that long, lean coach-driver lounging against the wall of the Customs building over there was not actually trying to make a pass at her—through the windows of the Buffalo-Toronto coach?

She stared at him, and saw his blond head jerk peremptorily at the building he was holding up as he gestured behind him with his thumb. No, not a pass, after all, she decided. Apparently he was telling her that she had to get off the coach and once again shuffle her way down the aisle to return to the Customs shed.

Sighing, Amber rose to her feet, mumbled an 'excuse me' to the middle-aged woman who was half asleep in the seat beside her, and, with what she hoped was a martyred expression on her face, made her way down the steps and over to the smiling blond man by the wall.

She blinked. His piercingly blue eyes were fixed on her with the sort of approving gleam that she was accustomed to seeing in the eyes of her fellow students—the male ones—when she wore a particularly revealing party dress. But she neither wanted nor expected this kind of appreciation from her coach-driver. Apart from which, she was wearing faded jeans and a baggy pink sweatshirt today, so there was no possible reason for him to look at her like that.

'What's the problem?' she asked coldly. 'Customs have already checked my bags and told me I can get back on the coach.'

'I know.'

'Then why...?'

He smiled, a long, lazy smile. 'I was bored. I wanted someone to talk to.'

Amber drew herself up to her full five feet five and pointed her small chin indignantly. 'Do you mean to tell me you got me off the coach just because *you*——'

'Wanted someone to talk to. That's right.'

His smile was teasing now, and she knew he was enjoying her indignation. She also took in for the first time that he was remarkably attractive.

When she had boarded the coach in Buffalo she hadn't really looked at the driver. And when they had reached the Canadian border point she had been so busy collecting her bags and convincing the Amazon behind the counter that she wasn't smuggling booze, jewellery or drugs that she had paid no attention to the driver who was shepherding his passengers efficiently through the bureaucracy. When Customs had finished with her she'd climbed thankfully back on board and closed her eyes.

It was only now, as she glanced at her watch and then at the smiling driver who was still leaning back with his ankles crossed and arms folded casually on his chest, that she realised they had been waiting almost an hour.

The driver. Yes, he was certainly worth looking at, even in the practical short-sleeved shirt and brown trousers of his uniform. Tall and tight-muscled, with broad shoulders atop a taut, sinuous body... His face was almost aquiline, with gleaming white teeth beneath a straight nose and very clear blue eyes which matched the sky. Nice. And his eyebrows were well-shaped and surprisingly dark. To top it all off, this unlikely vision of glorious manhood was crowned by a mane of wavy blond hair that might have been the envy of a Greek god.

And a golden-brown tan to set off the rest of him, thought Amber half resentfully. Very colourful. Although his face was really too narrow to be handsome, and his lips were a bit too thin. There was something about them, though...

'Penny for them.' Through a curiously physical fog, she heard the underlying amusement in his arrestingly sensuous voice.

'What?'

'Penny for them. Your thoughts.'

'Oh. I—I was just thinking.' Yes, she was thinking all right. About her sudden ridiculous urge to touch his hair. She swallowed hastily and searched for something to say. 'What's taking us so long?'

The driver sighed and leaned his head against the wall. 'Those noisy kids from Toronto. The ones with all the brand new basketball equipment.'

'What about them?'

'Lack of common sense, mainly. If people must smuggle, they'd be doing everyone a big favour if they'd do a thorough job of it.'

'That sounds like a lack of responsibility on your part,' said Amber loftily.

'Does it now?' He grinned. 'You must be a very highly principled young woman.'

Amber frowned and didn't answer, feeling that somehow she had been put at a disadvantage. When it became obvious that the silence was discomfiting her much more than it was him, she demanded almost sulkily, 'How come the basketball players are holding us up?'

'Because the silly young idiots didn't know enough not to flaunt all their booty in front of the Customs officials. They look so squeaky clean and shiny that any Customs officer would have to be fast asleep not to know they were bringing back more than they're allowed. Result—they've gone through every piece of the kids' baggage with a fine-tooth comb, and of course they all owe duty, which most of them haven't got.' He shrugged. 'There's a lot of high finance and wheeling and dealing going on in there now, I believe, while they try to scrounge up enough to pay the charges. Meanwhile the rest of us just have to sit here and wait.'

'Oh, I see. Not very bright of them.'

'Not very.' His eyes were laughing at her. 'But a mistake I presume *you'd* be much too clever—and highly principled—to make. Which college do you go to, by the way?'

Amber gaped at him. 'University of Manitoba. How did you know...?'

'Ah. Winnipeg. I thought so. And I knew because you look and sound like a student. U. of M.'s a good college.'

'How would you know?'

He raised his eyebrows. 'Shouldn't I?'

'Well, I mean, you're...'

'Right. I'm a coach-driver, aren't I, Miss College Student? And coach-drivers aren't supposed to know about universities.'

'I didn't mean——'

'Oh, yes, you did.' The look he gave her now was hard, and just a little contemptuous. 'That's exactly what you meant, and you know it.'

Yes, she supposed she did know it. But how could she be expected to guess he had a college education? *If* he had one. She opened her mouth to see if she could find some way of getting her foot out of it, but was rescued by a surge of tall and noisy youths from inside the Customs building. Laughing loudly, and pushing each other, the liberated basketball players tumbled aboard the bus.

'You'd think they would be a bit subdued, wouldn't you?' remarked the driver with resignation.

Amber realised that he was coolly smoothing over an awkward moment for her, and was grateful. Grateful and at the same time resentful. She wouldn't have been in a position to make tactless remarks in the first place if he hadn't ordered her off the coach—and under completely false pretences, as it had turned out.

A few minutes later they were on their way. The middle-aged woman next to her was now definitely asleep and snoring gently, and the disconcerting driver was safely behind the wheel at the front of the coach.

Amber closed her eyes, and in a very short time they were pulling into the coach-depot in Toronto.

'Amber! You look so—so grown-up. What a sight for sore eyes you are. My goodness, you've even grown taller!'

'Oh, Aunt Minnie, I couldn't have. I stopped growing when I was eighteen.' Amber jumped down the last step of the coach without even noticing that the driver's hand was extended to help her, and flew into the welcoming arms of her aunt.

'But, dear, we haven't seen you for over five years,' Minnie expostulated, laughing, as she returned her niece's enthusiastic hug.

'Has it been that long? Yes, I suppose it has.' Amber turned quickly to collect her two large suit-cases, and saw that the coach was now empty—and that the driver was standing behind her with his dark brows raised in enquiry.

'Yours?' he asked, pointing at the only two bags remaining on the platform.

'Yes. Thank you.' Amber reached to pick them up, but he was there before her, hoisting the two cases easily, as if they contained feathers instead of eight pairs of shoes, a hair-dryer, her jewel case, a trav-elling iron and all the clothes she had been able to squeeze in.

'Where to?' he demanded brusquely.

'Oh, that's all right. I can manage them,' began Amber. She certainly didn't want to be under any ob-ligation to this man, of all people—although in fact she *had* been wondering how she was going to manage the load, which now included presents she had ac-quired in Buffalo as well as everything else.

'Where to?' he repeated, not bothering to ac-knowledge her objection.

Oh, all right. If he wanted to be arrogant and dic-tatorial—and helpful—who was she to prevent him?

'Are we taking a taxi, Aunt Minnie?' she asked, averting her eyes carefully from the man who con-tinued, most irritatingly, to remind her of a Greek god.

'Yes, dear. Your Uncle Marty's at work and I'm afraid I still don't drive.'

'You should learn. It's easy.'

'Maybe it is for you bright young things, dear, but——'

'I know. You can't teach an old dog——'

'Your aunt is neither old nor a dog, Miss College Student,' said the driver, smiling wickedly at Amber's sixty-year-old, smartly dressed aunt. 'I'll take these to the taxi-rank for you, shall I?'

'Thank you. That would be very kind,' replied Minnie graciously, returning his smile with a twinkle.

And of course *I* should have been the one to say that, thought Amber crossly. She'd had precisely two very brief conversations with this man, and both times he had put her in the wrong.

All the same, as she and Minnie trotted behind him it was impossible not to notice what a very striking figure he made. Even from behind. He really had incredibly long legs, and that uniform fitted so well. His fingers were long, too, curled around the handles of her luggage...

'Here we are, then.' The object of Amber's scrutiny swung the cases down beside the taxi-stand and straightened slowly. 'Enjoy your night in Toronto. And remember not to miss the plane.' He raised his arm in a gesture of farewell, and before Amber could open her mouth he was striding rapidly back to the depot.

He *would* have to say that, she thought indignantly. Just because I almost missed the bus in Buffalo when I went to buy that magazine...

It was not until they were already in the taxi and speeding through the busy streets of Toronto that it occurred to her that she hadn't told him she was catching a plane the next day——

'What a helpful and charming young man,' glowed her aunt, interrupting Amber's thoughts. 'Most unusual. It's so hard to find anyone willing to lend a helping hand these days, especially in stations and coach-depots.'

'Mmm,' murmured Amber abstractedly, and thinking that he wasn't charming at all. 'Aunt Minnie—how do you suppose he knew that I'm catching the plane to Thunder Bay tomorrow?'

'I expect you told him so, dear.'

'But I didn't.'

'I see.' Minnie gave Amber a quick look, as if she thought the journey from Buffalo had been rather too much for her niece. 'But you must have, mustn't you, dear? After all, the man can't be clairvoyant.'

Maybe not, thought Amber sourly, but he can certainly be very annoying. And mysterious. Not that there was much point in discussing him with her aunt, who obviously thought he was delightful—and that Amber was in need of a good sleep.

'And how is everything in Winnipeg and Buffalo?' asked Minnie a short time later, as they settled down to enjoy a cup of tea before Uncle Marty arrived back home from work.

Amber smiled and slipped her shoes off. It was lovely to be back in the old-fashioned, comfortable house where the whole family used to gather for Christmas years ago. Of course, that had been before her father's construction business had become so successful that he'd moved his wife and daughter to a luxurious modern house in Winnipeg's most exclusive suburb. After that he hadn't wanted to spend Christmas in Toronto with his sister and her accountant husband—or in Buffalo with his schoolteacher brother and his wife. He had said that, since they could now afford to enjoy holidays in style, there was no need to spend them with relations in overcrowded houses with only one bathroom, too few bedrooms and no bar. From then on they had gone to Hawaii or Europe or the Bahamas for Christmas—

and for a long time Amber had missed the cosy crackling fires, roast chestnuts and easy laughter of the earlier, simpler days. Now, years later, she too looked forward to more sophisticated holidays. Still, it was good to be back with her aunt again. If only for one night.

'Uncle Richard and Aunt Janet are fine,' she told the smiling woman sitting across from her in the flowery, over-stuffed chair. 'My cousins are fine, too. I had a great week with them all. It was nice of them to ask me to stay before I started my job in Thunder Bay.' She sighed. 'I wish I could stay longer with you and Uncle Marty, though.'

'I wish you could, too, but I do understand that the job is important to you, dear. I'm just happy that you can come for the night.'

Yes, you would be, thought Amber. Dear, undemanding Aunt Minnie. So unlike the aggressive, ambitious man in Winnipeg who was her brother and Amber's father.

'Mother and Dad send their love,' she said quickly, although she couldn't remember either of them having sent anything of the sort.

'Thank you, dear. And, of course, you must give them mine.' Minnie got up and moved briskly into the kitchen.

After a while Uncle Marty came home, and the three of them sat down to a vast, fattening meat dish, the like of which Amber hadn't seen for years. At home they had a cook, who was instructed to make sure the family diet was healthy and nutritious, with an abundance of raw green vegetables. As a result, her father was remarkably trim for a man nearing fifty-five and Amber and her mother both had perfect figures. They also shared the same coppery, red-gold hair, but Alida

Jones always dressed hers in a classic chignon, whereas Amber's fell in a thick cloud about her shoulders.

And that's exactly the difference between us, she thought to herself much later when, tired and suffering from indigestion, she finally stumbled into bed. Mother would never have let her hair down, even metaphorically, and allowed herself to eat so much lovely fattening food.

She smiled drowsily. It didn't matter. Tomorrow she would be a thousand miles from Aunt Minnie's wonderful cooking.

But when she waved goodbye to her aunt and uncle at the airport early the next morning, she was surprised to find herself brushing a small tear from her eye. And then another.

She tucked her travelling bag firmly under the seat, pulled out the magazine which had nearly caused her to miss yesterday's coach, wiped away a third surreptitious tear, and settled down determinedly to read. After all, she was off to her new job at the Flatrock Lake Amethyst Mine at last, it was a bright and beautiful day, and there was no reason whatsoever for her to cry.

Amber was so busy concentrating on her positive thinking that it was not until they touched down in Thunder Bay that she noticed a shining blond head across the aisle that looked surprisingly familiar.

She swallowed. It couldn't be.

But as she rose from her seat to leave the plane, the owner of the head rose too, and smiled at her. It was a long, lazy, curving smile that she remembered all too well.

'Hello, Miss College Student,' drawled an unmistakable voice. 'Well done. You *did* manage to make it to the plane on time.'

CHAPTER TWO

'WHAT...?' Amber tried to speak, discovered she was croaking like a frog with a hangover, and tried again. 'What are you doing here?' she managed to choke out.

'Eventually I hope I'm driving to the Flatrock Lake Amethyst Mine,' he replied, glancing disgustedly at the shuffling passengers ahead of them. 'Assuming we ever succeed in getting off the plane.'

Amber noted that patience was not, apparently, one of this particular blond god's virtues. Then she stopped wondering if he had any, as the implication of his words sank in.

'You're going where?' She knew she was croaking again.

'To the Flatrock Lake Amethyst Mine,' he repeated blandly.

'But...but that's where *I'm* going. I have a summer job in the gift shop there.'

'I know.'

'But you can't possibly... Who *are* you, Mr...?' Amber was rarely speechless, but her words trailed off and she found she had nothing to say.

'My name's Maki. Kyle Maki. And you may call me Kyle, Miss Amber Jones.'

Without Amber being aware of it, they had somehow reached the terminal. Now she glanced up at the tall man striding beside her in tight black denims and a white sweatshirt—and she gulped.

'Maki,' she repeated slowly. 'Spelt M-A-K-I?'

17

'That's right.'

'Oh.' Things began to fall into place. 'Then you must be... I suppose you're connected with the Makis who own the mine?'

'As a matter of fact I am. Reijo and Helvi Maki are my parents.'

'They are? You mean... You mean you're their son?'

Kyle raised his eyes to the fluorescent ceiling. 'It usually works that way, I believe. Although at the moment I'm not sure they think that producing me was any particular achievement.' He grinned, and Amber was struck again by the surprising attraction of his thin-lipped mouth. She wondered what it would feel like... Yes, well, that was quite enough of that, wasn't it? What she had to do now was get to the bottom of this surprising man's presence on her plane. Amber didn't like mysteries, especially when they seemed to be connected with herself.

A few minutes later Kyle had collected her two large suitcases, plus a canvas travelling bag of his own, and was striding across the car park towards a long grey car.

'Wait a minute,' gasped Amber, trotting unwillingly in his wake. 'Wait a minute, Mr... Kyle. Mr and Mrs Maki said they'd be sending someone to meet me.'

He turned slightly but didn't break his stride. 'Right. I'm the someone. Fortunately we were travelling on the same plane.'

Amber could think of several words which would cover her opinion of this situation. 'Fortunately' was not one of them. But there seemed very little point in saying so, so she didn't answer, and when Kyle unlocked the door of the grey car she sank resignedly on to the seat.

'Do you always keep transportation parked conveniently at the airport?' she asked as Kyle swung his long legs underneath the wheel.

He gave her an oblique look and shook his head. 'Hardly. I expect Erik drove it in from Flatrock, and his wife Rose drove in behind him to take him home. Erik works with Dad out at the mine.'

'I see. Wouldn't it have been easier just to meet you—meet us?'

'Not from Rosie's point of view. This way she gets to shop in Thunder Bay. Maybe even persuade Erik to take in a movie before they head for home.'

'Oh.'

As they pulled away from the airport he asked suddenly, not looking at her, 'Why were you crying? When you first got on the plane?'

'I wasn't crying.'

'Yes, you were. That's why I left you alone.' His voice was unexpectedly gentle.

Amber shrugged and stared out of the window. 'Maybe I was a little. It was nothing. Just that I hadn't seen my aunt and uncle for a long time and it was tough to say goodbye. That's all.'

'Mmm. Can't they come to visit you in Winnipeg?'

'Yes, but they haven't for ages. I don't think they feel very comfortable——' She broke off abruptly, and turned startled eyes up to his. 'Aunt Minnie says you're not clairvoyant—but you seem to know an awful lot about me.'

He smiled. 'Not an awful lot, Miss . . . Can I call you Amber?' His voice curled around her name and made it sound like music. Rich, passionate music that was doing strange things to her pulse.

'Yes, of course,' she whispered, trying to look cool, but knowing she sounded breathless and over-whelmed—and very warm.

'Well, then, Amber, as a matter of fact my parents asked me to look out for you in Buffalo yesterday. I gather you'd told them you were arriving via the States. So you're quite right. I'm not in the least clairvoyant.'

'I see.' Amber was scowling now, annoyed with herself because Kyle, who seemed suddenly amused, was having such a disconcerting effect on her pulse-rate.

'What's so funny?' she asked grumpily.

'You. You look like a fluffy little kitten who's about to sharpen her claws against my thigh.'

Hastily banishing visions of doing anything re-motely connected with Kyle's thigh, Amber turned away from him and glared across the flatness of the town which had once been called Fort William before it joined up with neighbouring Port Arthur to become the much more romantic-sounding Thunder Bay.

'Don't sulk, kitten.' His voice was warm and teasing.

'I'm not!' snapped Amber. She continued to glare through the window for a moment, then added, 'I don't see why you didn't tell me who you were when we met on the coach yesterday. I *know* you knew I was me, because you said I looked like a student. And you didn't even bother to introduce yourself,' she complained.

'Oh, is that what's eating you?' Kyle laughed without mirth. 'If you really want to know, kitten, I didn't introduce myself at the border because I had a definite impression that you thought hob-nobbing with drivers was beneath you.'

Amber was silent. She didn't want to talk to this horrible man who called her kitten—or Miss College Student—any longer. He might be lovely to look at, and she was uncomfortably conscious of his body seated so close to hers, but he was also supercilious and annoying and—she had to admit it—he had a habit of making her feel like a silly, inexperienced child. Which she wasn't. Well—not a child, at least.

After a long while she spoke again. 'I don't see why you're here, anyway,' she said ungraciously. 'I mean, why aren't you off driving your coach somewhere?'

'In my proper place?' The blue eyes which matched the sky were suddenly narrowed.

'No, of course not. I didn't mean that at all.' For a moment Amber wished she could stand up and stamp her feet. Then she discovered that her wish was likely to be granted as Kyle wrenched the wheel sideways and swerved to the side of the highway to pull up beside the statue of a one-legged man which had appeared suddenly out of nowhere. Without a word he climbed out of the car and came round to open her door.

'Right,' he said crisply. 'Out you get.'

Oh, dear. Her thoughtless remark must really have made him angry.

'I didn't mean it,' she said again. And then as he stood there, implacable, 'Why do I have to get out?'

'In order to further your education. Which, I may say, leaves a lot to be desired.'

Amber thought even more seriously about stamping her feet, but she had a feeling that if she did this long-limbed devil who was pulling her up beside him would have his own methods of making her behave. Methods she wouldn't care for at all.

'What are you going to educate me about, then?' she asked suspiciously.

'This.' He waved his arm, and Amber followed the direction of his eyes and realised that she was looking out over the blue-grey waters of Lake Superior, to the distant formation of a peninsula.

Perhaps Kyle wasn't angry after all.

'The Sleeping Giant,' he explained, making sense of the odd-shaped protrusion which did indeed resemble the reclining form of some long, ungainly giant. When he saw that Amber was now looking more interested than suspicious, he added, 'He's supposed to be Nanabijou, who was turned to stone by the Ojibwa's Great Spirit when the white man discovered his secret silver mine.'

'He's—it's—lovely,' whispered Amber, her grey-green eyes turning big and soft because of the beauty of the lake and the legend.

For the first time since he had met this pert young miss, Kyle began to think his parents might not have made such a mistake in hiring her after all. He placed a hand gently on her shoulder, and she smiled up at him. He saw that she had a sweet, soft mouth, too—when it wasn't parted to make snippy remarks about people who didn't please her. Such as himself.

He smiled back at her, and his fingers tightened slightly. Then the smile broadened as he noticed that her neck had flushed a delicate shade of pink.

'Come on,' he said softly. 'We'd better be getting on.'

Amber nodded. 'Yes. Thank you for stopping. I think I needed—the air.' She gestured at the impressive bulk of the statue they were parked beside as they settled back into the car. 'That's Terry Fox, isn't it?'

'Yes. His run came to an end just about here. I don't suppose you knew that.'

'As a matter of fact I *did* manage to pick up that fact in the course of my deficient education,' replied Amber with a return of her old tartness. But she was quiet for a while after that, thinking about the one-legged young man who had raised millions for cancer research by running across the country, and had then had to give up the fight when the dreaded disease had returned. Perhaps Kyle was right. There was a lot she didn't know—and could not begin to imagine.

Then all her goodwill vanished as Kyle's blue eyes fastened blandly on her face. 'You look almost confused, my dear,' he remarked innocently. 'Is it possible that there *are* a few things left you haven't learned?'

'Quite possible!' snapped Amber. 'Also, I'm not your dear.' She glared at the trees hurtling past on the highway, so that she wouldn't have to notice the small smile tugging at his mouth.

'No, I didn't think you were,' he agreed equably.

Amber sighed. 'What actually *are* you doing in Thunder Bay, Mr Maki?' Whatever it was, she hoped he wouldn't be doing it for long. A day spent in this man's company was quite enough to be going on with, and if he was staying for any length of time... She shuddered.

'Enjoying myself,' he replied, his eyes slanting sideways at her as he negotiated a curve with an expert flick of his wrist.

'I don't doubt it.'

Kyle laughed softly. 'Sharpening your claws again? If you really want to know, I'm not driving a coach conveniently out of your life because I happen to have a few weeks' holiday, which I'm going to spend with my parents.'

'At the Flatrock Lake Mine,' said Amber in a small, tight voice.

'I'm afraid so. Do you suppose you can put up with me, kitten?'

Amber heard the amusement which his words could not quite conceal, and her head snapped round so fast, she could feel a muscle pulling in her neck. 'It's your home, Mr Maki, so I don't have a choice, do I? And my name's *not* kitten. Or Miss College Student. It's Amber.'

'Amber.' He was doing it again. Turning her name into a soft and sensuous song. And, maddeningly, her stomach was turning soft, too. She could feel it. And this *had* to stop. Now. Apparently she was to endure several weeks of this irritating man's company, and the only way to get through them was to remain calm, practical, reasonably co-operative and, above all, coolly aloof.

'Do you enjoy driving a coach, Mr Maki?' she asked brightly, in what she hoped was her best social voice.

The blue eyes held a hint of mockery as he replied with equal superficiality, 'Thank you for your interest, Miss Jones. Yes, as a matter of fact, I do.'

'Oh,' said Amber, deflated. 'Umm—er—that's nice.'

He didn't answer, but continued to glance at her with those gleaming cobalt eyes which she was now absolutely sure were laughing at her—and she gave up. Social games were not going to work on Kyle Maki. Amber wondered what *would* destroy that cool, unruffled self-possession, and wished she might have a chance to find out. It would be satisfying to shatter this man's smooth complacency. Satisfying, and—yes, quite possibly exciting.

She shifted restlessly in her seat, fidgeted with the handle of her bag and stared fixedly out of the window. She still had to travel the rest of the way to Flatrock Lake with this attractive and disturbing man, and, if she couldn't find some safe, conventional topic of conversation, it was going to be a tense and uncomfortable journey. For her, anyway. Though, from the way Kyle was lounging back against the seat with one hand on the wheel and the other resting loosely on his thigh, she didn't think he had a tense bone in his body.

'What made you take a job in the amethyst business?' he asked casually, suggesting exactly the safe sort of topic she needed.

'Oh,' she said quickly, trying not to show her relief, 'that's easy. I'm studying gemology as well as English, so I wanted to find some kind of related work for the holidays. As a matter of fact, I've never had a summer job before.' She sighed. 'My father didn't really want me to take one this year, either.'

'Why not? I understood he was the one who arranged this business with my parents.'

'Yes, he did. But that's because I insisted I was going to do *something*. He wanted me to go to Europe again, you see. He said I didn't need to work.'

'Lucky you.'

She glanced at his face, suspecting sarcasm, but it was totally without expression.

'I'm not as lucky as all that. My father had an idea ... I mean, he wants me to have the right education and the right background so that I'll meet all the right people and marry the right man.'

Kyle turned his head to look at her, and for once his eyes were not amused. 'And isn't that what you want, too—Amber?'

Amber shook her head. 'Not yet. Probably one day, if I love him and if he *is* the right man. But...' She laughed nervously, feeling suddenly embarrassed. 'But first I want to find out what life's like out there in the working world. And I also want a chance to use my brain. I do have one, you know.'

'Good for you.' He sounded as though he meant it. 'So I suppose you convinced your father that you intended to get a job in spite of him—and he decided he'd better find one for you that was—suitable?'

'How did you know?'

Kyle smiled, a little grimly. 'I met your father once. He came up to Thunder Bay for the fishing, and combined business with pleasure by making a deal with my father. The mine provides him with stone for fireplaces, decorative walls and so forth.'

Amber nodded. 'Yes, I know. He uses a lot of amethyst in his business. It's very popular in some circles. But you're right. Dad did want to be sure that I worked somewhere he could approve of——'

'And he'd met my parents, knew they often hired students for the gift shop in the summer—and didn't think there was much chance of your meeting unsuitable people way out here in the bush.'

Amber laughed ruefully. 'That's about it.'

'Mmm.' Kyle stretched an arm behind her neck, making her shiver. 'I suppose he didn't remember about me,' he murmured thoughtfully.

'If he did, I doubt if he'd consider you a threat,' replied Amber drily—and thinking, as Kyle returned his hand to its rightful place on the wheel, that if her father *had* thought that, he had been dead wrong.

'No,' said Kyle, 'of course not. He'd hardly expect you to be seduced by the driver of a coach, who is old enough——'

'You've got a royal chip on your shoulder about that coach, haven't you?' interrupted Amber. 'And you're *not* going to tell me you're old enough to be my father.'

He smiled bleakly. 'No, but at thirty-four I'm old enough to know better. And no, I don't have a chip on my shoulder about my job, but I was under the impression that you had. The truth is, I love it, or I wouldn't do it. How old are you, Amber?'

'It's not polite to ask a lady her age.'

'Nonsense. You're much too young to be a lady.'

He was laughing at her again. It was infectious, and Amber found herself laughing back. 'I'm twenty-two,' she admitted.

'A mere child.'

'I'm *not* a child,' objected Amber, who was not yet old enough to be flattered.

But Kyle was looking at her with a very odd glint in his eyes. Then his dark lashes covered them and she could no longer see their expression as he concentrated on the road. 'No,' he said slowly. And if he had been anyone else she would have sworn that he sounded surprised. 'No, you're not, are you?' His lids rose again and his eyes ran quickly over the slim body trapped securely behind its seat-belt. 'In fact, you're rather a lovely young woman. But I suppose you know that already.'

To her intense irritation, Amber blushed. 'Thank you, but I'm not at all lovely,' she protested. 'My father says I lack "presence".'

'Presence?' She saw the eyebrow closer to her slant upwards, and just for a moment his fingers touched the back of her head as he murmured softly, ' "Live hair that is shining and free"; not to mention big green eyes that frown too much, a funny, turned-up nose and a neat little chin that has a remarkable knack of pointing at me as if it belongs to a dowager duchess who has encountered a particularly nasty smell. You don't need "presence", Amber.'

'You had to spoil it, didn't you?' said Amber, not sure whether to laugh or hit him. First you quote Rupert Brooke at me—he's terribly dated, you know—then you tell me I have a funny nose and a duchess's chin—and now,' she added disgustedly, as she saw his shoulders begin to shake, '*now* you're laughing at me. Again.'

Kyle passed a hand across his mouth, and the gleam in the blue eyes was unmistakable. 'Sorry,' he replied, not sounding sorry at all. 'I'm afraid I can't resist it. Any more than you could resist letting me know that you recognised that quotation and considered me an old fogy for using it.'

'An old . . .' Amber was speechless. Anyone less of a fogy than Kyle Maki she was at a complete loss to imagine. At the moment she was also at a loss to imagine anyone whom she would more enjoy slugging where it hurt, but she reminded herself that he was driving, and that in any case violence was against her principles.

For the remainder of the forty-five miles or so to Flatrock Lake, Amber maintained a discreet silence, broken only by polite responses of one syllable when Kyle made some remark about the wooded countryside bordering the Nipigon Highway. She had come to the conclusion that silence was the only way to cope with the impossible man beside her, who, in spite of the fact that he was the sort of person her father would have regarded as a nobody, proved every time he opened his mouth—or she made the mistake of opening hers—that he was altogether somebody. All six feet whatever of gloriously masculine length of him . . .

Amber scowled again, and Kyle, who always seemed to be glancing in her direction when she wished he wasn't, noted the frown and remarked that she would look positively Neanderthal by the time she was forty if she didn't learn to improve her disposition.

Knowing he was right, Amber promptly replaced the scowl with an expression of studied blankness which she maintained all the way to the mine.

It left her feeling as if her face had been packed in mud and left to dry too long in the sun, but luckily Kyle drove very fast and it was only another twenty minutes before they turned off the highway and headed down a bumpy, partially gravelled road into the bush. Just when Amber had given up all hope of retaining the lunch she had consumed on the plane, the road widened into a large, tree-encircled clearing. On the other side of the clearing was a small, timbered cabin surrounded by several utilitarian-looking trailers, and beside it a long, low building displayed a sign in purple letters proclaiming it to be the Flatrock Mine Gift Shop. Obviously this was to be her place of business for the summer.

Kyle left Amber to extricate herself from the car while, with a resigned grimace, he shouldered her heavy bags again and headed for the timbered cabin.

By the time Amber caught up with him, the door had already been flung open and a rotund little woman with soft mousy hair, a round face and a short nose was trotting down the steps towards them.

'Mother,' smiled Kyle as he dropped Amber's luggage on to the hard-packed ground without ceremony and moved to enfold the little woman in his arms.

'Kyle!' She pushed him away and stared up at his face. 'Ah. I see the coach-driving agrees with you, after all. I was afraid you might turn all pale and pasty sitting behind that glass all day.'

'Not a chance.' Kyle shook his head. 'I spend too much time baking in the sun while my flock goes through Customs or stocks up on hamburgers and pop. I'm done to a turn, as you can see.'

Isn't he, though? thought Amber, taking in the golden tanned skin for the hundredth time that day and berating herself for the recurring urge she had to touch it, to run her fingers along the chiselled structure of his face...

But now Helvi Maki had turned away from her son and was directing a beaming blue gaze at Amber.

'You must be Amber,' she exclaimed. 'Forgive me, my dear, I didn't see you at first. My big son takes up so much space that sometimes it's hard to see around him.'

'Thanks, Mother,' murmured Kyle. 'You make me sound just like the Goodyear Blimp.'

'Some blimp,' muttered Amber as she moved past him to shake hands with her employer. But Helvi heard her, and laughed.

'Some blimp, indeed,' she agreed. 'I hope he's been looking after you, my dear. Come along in and I'll make you a good cup of coffee. Kyle, you take Amber's bags and put them in the white trailer.' She turned back to her new employee and added quickly, 'I hope you'll be comfortable in the trailer. I'm afraid there's very little room in our shack, and we thought you'd be happier on your own. Is that all right?'

'Of course it is,' Amber assured her. 'I'm grateful to you for having me at all, and I'm sure I'll be *very* comfortable in the trailer.'

'Good, good. And, of course, we're happy to have *you*. It gets very busy here in the summer, and the girl who used to help us has found a permanent job, so when your father phoned up it was like the answer to a prayer. Saved us all that advertising and interviewing, because with your background we know you're just the girl we need.'

As Amber followed Helvi into the cottage she tried not to think about the way Kyle's lips had twisted when his mother had mentioned her background—or the way his eyebrows had risen in what could only be described as disbelief.

The cabin, for all its small size, seemed entirely adequate for the two people who inhabited it. There was a bright, warm living-room filled with polished wood and autumnal chintzes, and the solid pine floor was covered by colourful rugs. A well-scrubbed kitchen overlooked the clearing, and Amber saw that there was a bathroom as well as a bedroom. Vaguely, she wondered where his parents managed to store Kyle when he appeared. His was not the sort of body one tucked neatly away in a corner. But perhaps one of the trailers was his. As long as it was not the one *she* was to occupy, she didn't foresee any problems.

Amber and Helvi had just settled down to their coffee when a tall figure loomed in the doorway. For a moment, with the sun behind him, Amber thought it was Kyle, then she realised that this man was dark, and although the finely chiselled features left no doubt as to the origin of Kyle's lean and attractive profile the newcomer was obviously in his fifties.

'My husband, Reijo,' beamed Helvi. 'Reijo, this is Amber.'

'Ah, you're here at last. It's good to meet you, Amber. Your father has been a customer of mine for years.'

Kyle's father seemed as pleased to see her as his wife had been, and his grey eyes were full of warmth and welcome as he came to shake Amber's hand. And that, she thought, is where the resemblance to his son ends. The only emotions Kyle ever seemed to show were mockery or contempt, at least as far as she was concerned.

Just then a shadow darkened the door, and a blond head ducked as the object of Amber's musings sauntered into the room.

'Reijo. Here's Kyle.' Helvi's voice was faintly accusing, as her husband sprawled in a chair without making any attempt to move.

'I know. We met outside.' There was something guarded in Reijo's voice now, and when Amber looked at Kyle she noticed for the first time the lines of strain around his eyes. There was tension in his shoulders, too, as he lowered himself on to a chair beside the table at which Amber supposed the family took its meals. From her vantage-point, Kyle seemed taller than his father, although they were probably about the same height.

Kyle's eyes flicked over to Amber. 'You and Dad have a lot in common,' he remarked enigmatically.

'Oh?' For some reason Amber wasn't sure she trusted the direction of this conversation, and she wasn't giving anything away.

But Reijo Maki returned his son's hard stare and remarked stonily, 'I'm sure we have. Miss Jones appears to have ambition.'

When Kyle didn't answer, Amber, embarrassed, interposed hastily. 'Your name—Maki. That's quite unusual, isn't it?'

'Not around here, it isn't,' replied Kyle flatly.

'Oh?' said Amber again, wondering why she should feel foolish.

'No, dear,' explained Helvi, bustling over with more coffee. 'Kyle's right. It's a Finnish name, you see. There's quite a large Finnish population in these parts.'

'Really?' said Amber, interested. 'I wonder why?'

'Because, Miss——' Amber glared at Kyle, who had taken over the conversation from his mother, so he continued with a smug little grin. 'Because, *Amber*, a lot of Finns came to Northern Ontario around the beginning of the century. Mostly for economic reasons, but of course the countryside here is a lot like Finland in a way. Endless lakes and forests.' He waved a long arm expansively. 'My grandfather worked in a lumber camp when he first arrived, and he said it was very like home.'

'How interesting,' replied Amber without enthusiasm. It *was* interesting, but she didn't like the way Kyle's eyes seemed to mock her.

'Isn't it?' he agreed evenly, leaning back in his chair and crossing one muscular leg over the other. 'Have we discovered something else you didn't know?'

'Of course you have. There's a lot I don't know, and you know it!' snapped Amber, forgetting for a moment the presence of Kyle's startled parents. 'And you can stop looking smug, Kyle Maki. It doesn't suit you a bit.'

'And I thought it did,' sighed Kyle, leaning back even further and putting his hands in his pockets. 'Ah, well, if I can't be smug, at least I can be superior.'

Amber, realising that the wind had been taken out of her sails, found her indignation abating. A reluctant smile was plucking at the corners of her mouth when Reijo said harshly, 'Superior? *You* think you have something to be superior about? Damn stupidity, I call it.' He lumbered to his feet and stamped off through the door, and Amber relinquished all thought of smiling as she looked anxiously at Helvi— whose round face had gone all blotched and crumpled—and then at Kyle, whose mouth was crooked and thinner than ever. And she saw that his lean face was very white and still, and that the long fingers which had touched lightly on her hair were now curled like talons on the edge of the table as he uncoiled his body and stood up.

For a moment his presence, as taut as strung wire, seemed to dominate the room. Then, with a well-chosen word which Amber hoped she hadn't heard right, he bent his head and stalked through the door behind his father.

'Oh, dear. And on his first day home, too. I was so hoping...'

Amber shifted her anxious gaze from the open door, and turned her attention to Kyle's mother, whose blue eyes were unhappily moist. 'Is there something I can do?' she asked doubtfully. When Helvi didn't answer, without thinking she got up, walked over to the older woman and put her arm around her.

At that Helvi did speak. 'No,' she murmured, 'there's nothing anyone can do with those two stupid great hulks. They're both so sure they're right, they can't see beyond the noses on their long, dumb faces.

And my Reijo's the more stubborn of the two of them because he's disappointed. He just can't accept that Kyle is a grown man.'

And how! thought Amber involuntarily. Aloud she said, 'I'm sorry. I wish I could help, but I don't even know what's—what's . . .'

'What's the matter with my stupid menfolk? I'm not sure I do, either. But if you want an answer to that, my dear, you'll just have to ask my son.'

CHAPTER THREE

'Ask my son,' Helvi had said. But even if she had wanted to, Amber didn't find an appropriate moment to ask Kyle such a question that night.

She finished her second cup of coffee hastily and told her hostess that she thought she ought to unpack. The only trouble with this perfectly reasonable idea was that when she had a chance to inspect her trailer, she discovered that the unpacking of her over-stuffed cases was going to be a major undertaking which would require considerable concentration. It was not something which could be sandwiched between daydreams and the confused musings on the subject of the Maki family which she had rather had in mind.

The trailer was small. A padded bench and a table converted to a bed which let down from the wall. There was a narrow cupboard for clothes, and another for dishes above a minute chrome sink beside a stove. An almost doll-sized bathroom contained basic necessities, no bath or shower, and two shelves. That, of course, was the problem. Everything was doll-sized and basic except her own extravagant conception of packing.

With a sigh, Amber set to work to stow everything away. She piled her shoes on the floor, put her makeup on one shelf in the bathroom, hung up as many of her clothes as she could cram into the cupboard and, in an uncharacteristic gesture of frustration, gave up everything else as a bad job to be put back in suitcases tomorrow and stored elsewhere—anywhere! In the meantime, she could throw the whole mess on the bed.

Amber liked her life, as well as her belongings, to be organised. People, too. Not that Kyle and his family would fit into her nice, identifiable compartments any more than her clothes would fit into the cupboard. Helvi, perhaps, was easy enough to understand, but the men were impossible to pigeon-hole. Kyle, she thought glumly, was maddening, amusing, infuriating and attractive all at the same time. And he confused her horribly. His father, who had seemed so easygoing at first, undoubtedly had a temper. And there was a tension between these two male creatures which she didn't understand at all, but which promised to make life very uncomfortable if hostilities were going to continue.

She sighed, put her brush and comb in the kitchen drawer, removed them again, and pulled open the cupboard over the sink. It was stocked with tins of soup and juice, packages of cereal, bread, and almost everything she might need for a quick meal. Bless Helvi. Even though she had insisted that Amber must have supper with the family every evening, she had made sure that her new employee wouldn't starve at any other time of the day.

When a knock came on her door some time later, Amber was staring through the small window of the trailer at two birds sitting immobile on the slender branch of a tree. One of them was singing. She didn't turn immediately, and before she knew it the door had burst open and the small space seemed to be completely filled with Kyle.

'Dreaming, Amber?' he asked softly, his mouth very close to her ear.

'No,' she replied firmly. 'I was watching those birds over there. Don't you ever wait to be asked before you come barging in?'

'Occasionally, I suppose. Although I rarely have to wait long. The birds are white-throated sparrows.'

He was staring at her with such deliberate provocation that Amber felt a furious urge to hit out. She was feeling other urges too, but those must be rigidly controlled. Especially in this small and intimate space, she realised as he took a step towards her.

She raised her hand, and Kyle caught her smartly by the wrist. Before she knew what had happened, he had drawn her to him so that she was pulled against his chest.

'I wouldn't try it if I were you.' He spoke very quietly and a shiver ran through Amber's body that had nothing to do with the iciness in his voice, and everything to do with the gentle pressure on her wrist and the feel of his hard body against her own. She could feel the tautness of his thighs, too—and his legs...

For a moment she couldn't breathe. Then she saw a faint gleam of what looked like triumph in his eyes, and her breath returned in a rush. 'You can stop leering at me, Kyle Maki. You'll have to wait till hell freezes over before *I* ask you in.'

Kyle released her arm. 'Winter comes early in these parts,' he remarked mildly. 'Some people say it's hell.'

But when Amber, pushed beyond her normal healthy sense of self-preservation, lifted her arm again and told him he was behaving like the arrogant, stupid lout that he was, he only laughed. 'We're back to that, are we?' he asked conversationally, as he caught her wrist with the same easy movement and held it loosely against his thigh.

'Back to what?' snapped Amber, trying to pull away and not succeeding.

'My congenital stupidity.'

'And bloody arrogance!'

Again he raised his eyebrows in that way that drove Amber mad. 'Such vehemence,' he chided.

'And such a big word to come from such a little mind,' shouted Amber, now completely beyond reason.

'I knew you'd be adorable when you were angry.' Kyle smiled complacently, and Amber felt angry tears prick her eyes. She had just lifted a foot to kick him when his face changed suddenly and he added, with what sounded like sincerity, 'I'm sorry, Amber. I never could resist teasing redheads. I only came because Mother told me to call you for supper.'

Amber bit her lip to keep from spitting at him, thought for a moment, and then enquired sweetly, 'Do you mean you actually do what Mother says?'

He grinned. 'It's as much as my life's worth not to. Come on, Amber. Let's call a truce and eat.'

His grin was suddenly so engaging that to her amazement Amber found her anger evaporating. Perhaps Kyle wasn't really so bad, after all. Anyway, she only had to endure another few weeks of his company. She wondered just how many weeks that would be.

'All right. Truce,' she said reluctantly.

When Kyle smiled and casually picked up her hand to lead her towards the cabin, she decided that in spite of everything that had happened, and in spite of Kyle's impossible personality, the next few weeks promised to be very—interesting. Interesting and—yes, maybe even enjoyable. Besides, she had always appreciated a challenge.

As Amber had anticipated, supper with the Makis was not a comfortable occasion.

Helvi fussed about serving huge portions of a very tasty stew and chatting brightly to Amber about the mine, how much work it was, and how glad they were that Reijo had decided to invest in it ten years ago when his prospecting hobby had finally promised to yield some tangible benefits.

'Yes,' said Kyle, his voice expressionless. 'Dad threw over a nice, safe accounting job in order to start up the mine.' He was looking at Reijo as he spoke, and there was something in the intensity of his gaze that Amber couldn't begin to understand. Something which smouldered dangerously beneath very bright blue ice.

Then she saw that the same banked fire was visible in Reijo's smoky eyes, and she wondered, not for the first time, about the cause of the surprising antagonism between these two overpowering men.

In a moment she was given a clue.

'At least I chose something with a future. Something I could be proud of. Proud to leave behind for my grandchildren.'

This time the look on Kyle's face was easy to interpret: impatience with a subject obviously debated many times before. 'You don't *have* any grandchildren, Dad,' he replied, through very white teeth. 'And even if you had the mine would probably be exhausted by the time they grew up.'

'Perhaps, but the profits wouldn't be. You're thirty-four years old, for heaven's sake. I was only twenty-five when you were born.'

'Now, Reijo,' expostulated Helvi. 'You can't expect Kyle to produce grandchildren for you until he has a wife.'

'Right,' agreed Kyle. 'And as no woman has yet shown the slightest inclination to share my life——'

'Nonsense,' said Helvi. 'Christina's a lovely girl. She's very fond of you.'

'Mmm. She's also fond of her career, and she's not remotely interested in marriage. We have a perfectly satisfactory arrangement—when we see each other, which isn't all that often any more.'

'Huh,' snorted Reijo. 'Of course it isn't. You're never in Toronto any more. Always on the road—in a *coach*.'

'Arrangement?' queried Helvi. 'Kyle, you know I don't approve... And in front of Amber, too.'

The faint resentment marring Kyle's attractive features vanished immediately at that, and his eyes lit with a wicked amusement. 'It's all right, Mother,' he assured her, his voice shaking suspiciously. 'I promise not to make any—arrangements—in front of Amber. I wouldn't dream of spoiling her innocence.'

'Kyle...' began Helvi severely.

'I'm not innocent...' began Amber indignantly. And then she remembered that she was.

There was an awkward silence for a moment, then suddenly she caught Kyle's eye. His lips twitched, she began to smile—and then both of them were laughing. Helvi, the disapproving tightness around her mouth receding gradually, looked from one grinning face to the other and joined in. For a while Reijo sat glowering at them all, but in the end he was no match for the hilarity around him and he too gave way to reluctant laughter.

For the first time that day, Amber began to feel happy and relaxed. Maybe the Makis did have their family differences, but beneath all the baiting and hard words they obviously cared for one another.

This summer was going to be all right, after all. She hoped.

After more of Helvi's excellent coffee, Amber said she thought that if she was to begin work tomorrow she had better get an early night.

'That's right, dear,' nodded Helvi. 'You get some sleep, and in the morning Kyle will show you around the mine. After that we'll start you in the shop.'

'Thank you,' said Amber as she bid them a smiling goodnight.

But almost her last thought before she dropped off to sleep was that another tête-à-tête with Kyle was not a prospect calculated to promote a good night's sleep—and not at all the way she would have chosen to start her first day on the job. Vaguely, she also remembered hearing the name Christina, and wondered why for some reason she didn't like it. Christina. It was a perfectly harmless name. Pretty, even, but... No, she didn't care for it one bit.

When Amber felt the first warm rays of sun on her face in the morning, she stretched lazily, turned over, and immediately went back to sleep. Vaguely, in her dreams, she thought she heard knocking, but the next thing she knew for sure was that there was a very peculiar scraping noise coming from beside her window. She turned her head slowly, and now her only thought was that it wasn't the prospect of a tête-à-tête with Kyle Maki which disturbed her, but the likelihood of his imminent eruption into her sleeping quarters.

A brown, muscled arm extended through the window which Amber had left open, and long fingers were grasping at the handle of the door which, out of habit and many nights spent in hotel rooms, she had automatically locked the night before. Not that she had supposed there was much need to lock doors in this out-of-the-way spot. Still, you never knew. Perhaps marauding bears were not the only animals which wandered this part of the world. Anyway, if she guessed right, at the moment she had more to fear from wolves—one wolf, to be exact, with white teeth and golden-blond hair.

As Amber's mesmerised gaze fastened on the handle, it turned, slowly at first, then faster as the door sprang open with a jerk and just missed slamming into the wall.

She pulled the sheet well up under her chin and closed her eyes.

'Playing ostrich?' enquired a voice from above her head. 'It won't do you a bit of good, you know.'

Amber decided her only defence was to play possum, not ostrich, and went on doing her best impersonation of a corpse.

But when she felt the faint spiciness of male breath whispering across her cheek, and realised that a cool hand was tugging at the sheet around her neck, her eyelids flew open so rapidly that at first she was blinded by the sun.

'Hey! What do you think you're doing?' she yelped.

Kyle's mouth was not six inches from her own as he replied in a voice which obviously meant business, 'Getting you out of bed. Now. It's nearly ten o'clock, Mother's opening up the store, and I'm supposed to see you have breakfast and take a look around the mine.'

'Oh. All right. I'm sorry I slept so late.' Amber's eyes met his guiltily. 'I forgot to bring an alarm.'

'You're used to room service, I imagine,' he replied drily. 'If you like, I can always provide it.'

Kyle's heavy eyelids did not quite hide a gleam which Amber decided she didn't trust at all. 'Oh, no, you can't,' she said quickly. 'And you can take your hand away from my neck as well. If you don't mind.'

'It's not your neck I'm interested in, kitten.'

'Now just a minute——' began Amber indignantly.

'It's this sheet,' he explained innocently, pulling it down to her shoulders. 'I was planning to remove it. Just to encourage you to move your charming body out of that comfortable bed.'

'Don't you dare. And my body won't be charming at all. I couldn't find my nightdress last night and I haven't got any clothes on.'

'What a tempting proposition. Sounds charming enough to me.' The gleam was more pronounced than ever.

'Goose-bumps *aren't* attractive,' retorted Amber with conviction.

'Oh, I don't know——'

'Well, I do. Now will you please get out of here, Kyle Maki?'

'Not on your life. You'll just go back to sleep.' He kicked the door closed, leaned against it and folded his arms on his chest.

'I won't, I promise. I'll be out in ten minutes.'

Kyle straightened. 'All right. Ten minutes. But if you're one second longer I'm coming right back in here to give you six of the best on that promisingly bare behind.'

Amber glared at him. 'Out!' she spluttered. 'Out this minute.' Oh, if she could only get up and throw the nearest heavy object at his head. As she lacked a suitable blunt instrument, that pair of black hiking boots over there would do quite well.

But Kyle, smiling smugly, was already on his way to the door. 'Ten minutes,' he repeated as he pulled it closed behind him.

Once outside he paused, shook his head, and stared disbelievingly around him. Not even a tremor of a breeze was riffling the bright green foliage. Goosebumps indeed! On a breathless day like this. That snippy little chit in there must think he had cotton between his ears. But of course that was exactly what she did think, wasn't it? Miss Amber Jones had made very little effort to conceal her lack of respect for his mind. In fact, she took every opportunity to point out that he didn't have one. He smiled grimly. He'd known plenty like her in his time. Clever young things who thought a couple of years of higher education gave them a monopoly on all there was to know.

No, he amended now, moving slowly across the clearing. No, he hadn't known any *quite* like this one. She was a child, and a very spoilt one at that, and he wanted to treat her as such. Most of the time he succeeded. He couldn't resist teasing her, either, just as he might the spitting, pouncing kitten he sometimes called her. But still, she wasn't your average spoilt little rich girl. There was something about her— something spunky and rather endearing... And whenever he stopped to think about it, he was aware that she was also remarkably attractive. Back in the trailer a minute ago he had felt sensations stirring in his body that certainly had nothing to do with the childish aspects of Amber's personality...

Kyle pulled out a handkerchief and wiped it across his forehead. This day was going to be far too hot to even think about anything of that sort, and, anyway, she was much too young. *Much* too young, he repeated under his breath.

Poached eggs, that was what he would make them for breakfast. Yes. Eggs. He would concentrate on eggs.

His lips twisting in self-derision, Kyle strolled across the hard-packed earth and went into his parents' cabin.

Back in the trailer, Amber had thrown off the bed-sheet and was jumping hastily to her feet. She didn't believe Kyle's threats, and there was no way she would let him carry them out in any case, but she had no intention of giving him any excuse to come back through that door.

She groped frantically through the pile of clothes heaped on the end of her bed, pulled on yesterday's jeans and a clean blue T-shirt, remembered she hadn't washed and started again. Then a quick comb through her red-gold hair, a dash of lipstick . . . Oh. Shoes. She hadn't any shoes on. There they were, under-neath the hiking-boots. Pale blue running shoes with white laces. Oh, dear. Six minutes had gone already, and her trailer looked as if an earthquake had hit it. Or a very untidy young woman, which she wasn't. She thought wistfully of home, where the kind-hearted housekeeper was always around to clear up if she was in a hurry.

Amber frowned as her eyes fell on her nightdress, which was trapped between a sun-hat and a heavy tome on gemology. No wonder she hadn't been able to find it last night. Of course, there was too little space in this trailer, and she had brought far too much luggage—but this was ridiculous. Quickly she threw her remaining clothes on the floor, heaved the fold-away bed against the wall to reveal the small table and bench, slung the clothes back on to the bench again and hurried towards the door. Top marks for neatness she wouldn't get, but there would be time to clean up this devastation later.

Right now her main priority had to be bearding the blond wolf in his den—before he could beard her in hers.

Kyle was just shovelling eggs on to buttered toast on two blue-rimmed plates when Amber strolled through the door of the cabin, trying to look cool and casual and not in the least out of breath.

In her jeans and T-shirt the casual part was easy enough. Cool was harder because the day was becoming increasingly warm. But controlled breathing became utterly impossible as her green eyes encountered Kyle's blue ones. What *was* it about this thoroughly obnoxious man...? For a second, as the eyes which had caused her to catch her breath narrowed slightly, she thought he felt something, too. Then he was glancing pointedly at his watch.

'Hmm. Right on time,' he remarked non-committally.

'Disappointed?'

'No. Delighted. My parents don't need a Sleeping Beauty this summer.'

'Maybe a Cinderella, then?' suggested Amber acidly. 'With you as an Ugly Brother?'

Kyle stared at her, lifted his hand as though he intended to strike her, then threw back his head and laughed. *'Touché,'* he said lightly, pulling out a chair and gesturing at her to sit. 'Eat your eggs, Cinderella. Cooked with my own ugly hands.'

'Oh, your hands aren't——' began Amber. Then she saw that he was teasing her as usual, swallowed, and sat down.

'You're a good cook,' she told him a few minutes later. It seemed a safe enough topic, and indeed the eggs had been absolute perfection. Cooked just enough to set the yolks without making them rubbery or stiff.

'Not really,' replied Kyle with unexpected modesty. 'I can manage the basics because they're all I ever try.'

'Oh. Do you live alone, then?' As soon as the words escaped from her mouth she wished she hadn't spoken them, because Kyle was looking at her with that thin, curling smile again, and she could feel the colour flowing over her face.

'I didn't mean——' she began. And then stopped. What didn't she mean? That she suspected that Kyle lived with a woman called Christina? She stared hard at her plate, pushing her fork pointlessly over the remaining streaks of yellow.

And for once Kyle came to her rescue. 'Yes, I do live alone,' he told her matter-of-factly. I enjoy my own company most of the time, and when I do need someone——'

'When you do need someone—there's always Christina.'

Kyle looked startled. 'Christina? How on earth do you know——? Oh, yes, my mother mentioned her, didn't she?' He smiled without much amusement. 'Not much gets by you, does it, Miss Curiosity?'

'I couldn't help hearing. And I'm *not* especially curious. I was just making conversation.' Amber removed her nose from her plate and stuck it in the air.

It wasn't true, though. Her curiosity had always been both a blessing and a curse. Blessing, because her passion for facts and her desire to know *why* and *what* had ensured her excellent marks at school, which had meant that her self-made father, who thought education was a waste of time for women, had been unable to resist the pressure to send her to university. Curse, because her obsessive need to know what made things—and people—tick often landed her in hot water when friends thought she had crossed the barrier between healthy curiosity and sheer nosiness.

As Kyle was undoubtedly thinking now.

But, surprisingly, he seemed to accept her statement that she couldn't help hearing Helvi's comments. He picked up his plate, rinsed it under the tap, and came back to collect hers.

'OK,' he nodded. 'Point taken. Mother does have a fixation about Christina. I brought her home for the holidays once, and my parents have had us at the altar ever since.'

'But you're not...?'

'No. We're not. We're friends, and sometimes— more than friends.' He smiled reminiscently. 'But that, my dear incurious Amber, really *is* none of your business.'

It could have been a rebuke, but somehow the way he said it was friendly, almost as if he were sharing something with her, and Amber found herself smiling.

'You're quite right,' she agreed cheerfully. 'Come on, let's clean up these dishes and get on. We mustn't keep your mother waiting any longer than we have to.'

'Good girl,' said Kyle approvingly. 'That's what we need around here. Energy and enthusiasm.' He turned on the tap and accidentally splashed hot water on Amber's bare arm.

'Watch it, Torquemada,' she protested. 'I promise to work without the water torture. There'll be no Sleeping Beauties at Flatrock.'

'No Sleeping Beauties,' he agreed solemnly. 'Make with the dishcloth, Cinderella.'

*   *   *

'Good morning, Mr Maki.' Amber waved as she and Kyle passed by Reijo, who was seated high in the cab of a front-end-loader and lighting a cigarette.

Without looking up, Reijo waved back, but it was obvious that he was much more interested in the activities of his loader as it shifted a pile of purplish rubble across the quarry than he was in the presence of Amber and his son.

'Dad always gets going early,' explained Kyle. 'And, as you can see, he is not at all easily distracted.'

'Good for him,' said Amber.

'Mmm. I suppose it is. Good for him, I mean.' He picked up a coloured stone and tossed it absently at a large boulder. 'I suppose you don't know much about the mining process, do you, Amber?'

'I should,' she replied, unable to disguise her satisfaction at being able to contradict him. 'After all, I have studied gemology.'

'Of course. Which makes you an expert,' murmured Kyle, raising his eyes to the treetops and immediately making Amber wish that one of them would fall conveniently on his head.

'*Actually,*' she continued in her haughtiest voice, 'amethyst is only a variety of quartz, isn't it? And the mining is done on a rather small scale, I imagine—and only in the summer.'

'Which puts me and mine in suitably insignificant perspective,' remarked Kyle drily. 'And yes, if you imagine there are no dramatic explosions and showers of rocky fireworks, you're absolutely right. We drill shallow holes and use low-power explosives, just enough to blast open the rock in the hope of finding quality gemstones.' He ran a hand casually round the back of his neck. 'But, of course, most amethyst is massive because the crystals have grown together. We ship out granite faced with amethyst to the construction industry. It's used for fireplaces, patios, tabletops——'

'I know,' interrupted Amber. 'There's no need for the lecture. My father is in the construction business, remember?'

For a moment Kyle's hard gaze held her in a vice. Then he smiled and said evenly, 'So he is. Which is why we have the pleasure of your company.' The smile was genuine, for once untainted by sarcasm.

So her rudeness about the scale of his family's business had apparently been forgiven. Amber decided the local trees could hold off a while before falling on his head.

Kyle took her hand and led her up a rock-strewn slope to the bottom of a low granite cliff. 'This is where most of our tourists like to come rockhounding,' he explained. Then he temporarily abandoned his role of tour-guide to admire the enchanting picture presented by Amber's neat denim behind as she bent over to pick up an attractive reddish-brown stone shot through with streaks of purple.

'Isn't it lovely?' she cried, straightening quickly to hold out her new-found treasure.

Kyle studied her eyes, which appeared to have changed from greyish-green to violet. To his mind, they reflected the beauty of the stone she held in her hand. 'Yes,' he said. 'Very lovely.'

Amber wondered why her cheeks felt suddenly hot. '"All bright and glittering in the smokeless air..."' she murmured hurriedly, because she had to say something and, for some obscure reason, they were the first words that came into her head.

'Nonsense. For one thing, the air is hardly smokeless,' said Kyle dampingly, waving a hand at his father who was still pulling on a cigarette. 'For another, Wordsworth was talking about buildings.' He turned away from her, and Amber couldn't understand why his voice was suddenly gruff.

'You're a very strange man,' she said to his rigid back. 'Are you always so deflating?'

'When it's necessary.' He turned to face her again, and now his expression was disconcertingly blank.

'And with me it's always necessary, I suppose,' she replied resignedly, wondering why his opinion of her mattered.

'No. Not always. You have your points.' Kyle made a determined effort to keep his eyes off the point he had in mind. 'Come on. I'll show you our amethyst cave.'

He led her across the quarry to an area where he said blasting had exposed a vug, or cavity, which was proving a spectacular success as a tourist attraction.

A small opening led into what was almost a minute room, although the roof was too low for Kyle to be able to stand upright. The floor was of a reddish clay which sparkled with tiny chips of violet, and the walls were lined with pointed clusters of amethyst so large that Amber could cover them with her hand.

'Oh!' she gasped. 'I didn't think it was possible. Imagine all this, forming over millions of years, and then your father happening to uncover it . . .'

'Mmm. He was prospecting for silver or zinc at the time, I think. Then he noticed a vein of amethyst on a ridge not far from the lake.'

'Oh, yes,' said Amber, running a hand across the shimmering rockface. 'The lake. Where is it? I haven't seen it yet.'

'Just over that bluff on the other side of Dad and his loader.' He put his head on one side and grimaced. 'And since I think we're about to be invaded by the State of Minnesota on the march, I'll take you over there now before we're trapped.'

A moment later, as Amber scrambled back through the opening of the cave, she was almost knocked down by a party of middle-aged ladies in bright red trouser-suits. All except two of them were chattering in loud, excited voices—and the two exceptions were singing.

'They'll all start off in a minute,' Kyle warned her. 'We've had ladies' choir groups before.'

'Very appropriate,' laughed Amber. 'This place makes me want to sing, too. Oh.' She paused. 'Who's that with them? He doesn't look like part of a ladies' choir.'

'No, and he wouldn't thank you for suggesting it. That's Erik. He works here and does most of our tours for us. He can't stand tourists,' added Kyle indifferently.

'Isn't he in the wrong job, then?' asked Amber, glancing sideways at the grim-faced, dark young man who seemed to be saying something about Dionysus in a loud, rather bored voice.

'Probably, but then most people are.'

'Including you?'

'No. Not including me.' Kyle's reply was curt to the point of rudeness.

'You've reached your full potential, then, have you?' enquired Amber sweetly.

As Kyle's deep blue eyes lit with the threat of retribution, she skipped hastily ahead of him and headed for the top of the bluff.

About half a mile away, the pale turquoise waters of Flatrock Lake sparkled in the morning sun. Amber gazed down at it, entranced, thinking that the wide sandy beach at the bottom of the path leading down from the bluff would be a perfect place to sunbathe—if she ever had the time. It was a very flat beach and the sand, with its bleached white logs, looked warm and inviting.

She smiled and drew a long, pleasurable breath. Then the smile was wiped from her face. She felt long fingers circle the back of her neck as a low voice whispered threateningly in her ear, 'You shouldn't stand so close to the edge, young lady. Sometimes temptation is very hard to resist. Especially when the provocation is—substantial.'

'Oh!' squealed Amber, trying to turn her head to look up at him, and finding that she couldn't move it. 'Oh. You wouldn't—would you?'

'Probably not,' replied Kyle laconically. 'I doubt if it's steep enough to do you sufficient damage.'

'Thanks a lot. I do wish you'd let go of my neck.'

Abruptly Kyle did as he was asked, and Amber was irritated to find that she almost regretted losing the touch of his fingers on her skin. Damn. This man was going to be a problem.

She glanced up at him quickly and saw that he was grinning at her. 'I suppose you think you're clever,' she muttered crossly.

'Reasonably.'

'Well, I *don't*!' Again Amber had to resist an urge to stamp her feet.

'Mmm. So you've mentioned. On numerous occasions.'

'Oh, you—you——!'

Kyle raised his eyebrows. 'Rat? Bastard? Toad?' he suggested obligingly.

'*All* of them!' shouted Amber, turning away from him and taking the nearest escape route she could find—which happened to be the winding, wooded path which led down to the lake.

Behind her she heard a snort of masculine derision. Clamping her lips shut, and then opening them again because she was out of breath, Amber increased her speed so that her feet were just skimming over the pathway, and in a very short time she had reached the edge of the sand.

She paused for a moment, taking in the pale, still water which stretched some distance across to the wooded shore opposite. It looked cool. And she was hot for more reasons than one. A quick paddle might relax her, soothe the raw edges of her nerves . . .

Yes. Amber made up her mind, and with quick, determined strides she began to walk past a wall of logs which seemed to be embedded in the sand.

She had only taken a few steps when she realised that her blue running shoes were sinking. She stared down at them. Oh, well, it must be a bit marshy just here at the edge of the trees. She could easily wash the shoes. She advanced a little further, and without warning her footwear disappeared completely. So did her ankles.

'Help!' yelled Amber. 'Kyle, help. I'm sinking!'

There was a movement behind her and she turned thankfully to greet her rescuer. Then relief changed to shock as she sank into the mud up to her knees and saw that it was not Kyle who stood beside her ready to pull her out, but a very large moose who was passing not four feet away.

He ambled regally past her struggling figure, headed out a little way, stared thoughtfully at the lake—and then started to amble back.

CHAPTER FOUR

'KYLE!' shrieked Amber again. 'Kyle, come quickly!'

Her feet seemed to have touched bottom at last, but she was caught fast to her knees in the oozing muck. The moose, who seemed oblivious to the mud sucking at his legs, glanced at her and resumed his stately progress towards the woods.

'Amber? What is it?' Round a bend in the path Amber saw the top of Kyle's fair head, and she thought that she had never seen a more welcome sight in her life.

'Help!' she cried. 'Oh, Kyle, help me. I'm stuck. And there's a moose . . .'

At the edge of the mud Kyle came to a startled halt. 'Hell!' he exclaimed. Then, as his eyes took in Amber's mud-caked figure scrabbling frantically in the bog for the running shoes which had been sucked off her feet, he threw back his head and let out such a shout of laughter that the moose, disconcerted, gave them a disgruntled look and disappeared into the trees.

Amber straightened slowly. Her shoe hunt had been unsuccessful, and now she was covered in brown goo up to her elbows. Kyle stood only a foot or two away from her, grinning his white-toothed grin from ear to ear and making not the slightest attempt to help her out.

'If you'll just hang on a second, I'll fetch my camera,' he suggested helpfully.

'Don't you dare!' shouted Amber. 'Help me out, you——'

56

'Toad?'

'*Yes*. Can't you see I'm stuck?'

'Of course I can. That's why I want my camera.'

'Kyle Maki, I'm stuck in this filthy muck, I've lost my new running shoes, and if you don't help me out this minute, I'll—I'll . . .' Her face crumpled.

Help, thought Kyle. If I don't get her out this minute she's going to burst into tears. And quite suddenly, funny as the situation was, he knew that he didn't want to make her cry.

'Here,' he said, bending his tall body and extending a muscular arm. 'Grab my hand and heave.'

Amber grabbed, Kyle leaned backwards, and, with a slight popping sound like small balloons exploding, the marsh released her ankles and she was free.

'Oh!' she gasped, her mud-stained body falling against the whiteness of his shirt. 'Oh, Kyle. I thought I was trapped there forever, and then when that moose wandered out so close to me——'

'He wouldn't have bothered you.' His voice was soothing now, though it still held an edge of amusement, and his arm held her mud-stained body quite gently against his chest.

'Wouldn't he? I don't know much about them.' Amber tried to control the quiver in her throat.

'A real city girl, are you? No summer camping trips to the lake?'

'No. Dad went fishing sometimes, but Mother and I always stayed home. When he took *us* with him, it was different. Then he liked to travel around the globe.'

Kyle's lips quirked. 'And his idea of travelling didn't include moose?' he queried.

'No. It didn't include quicksand, either,' said Amber with a touch of asperity.

'I didn't think so. It's not really quicksand, you know. But, my dear girl, you must have seen all the logs and debris half-buried in the bog. Didn't that tell you anything?'

'No,' said Amber in a small voice, resting her cheek briefly against his chest.

As Kyle shook his head and moved his arm down her back, she suddenly became conscious that she was standing on the edge of this very unpleasant lake in the arms of a man she was particularly determined to dislike, and that he was holding her rather too closely. Also, his white shirt was now liberally smeared with mud.

'I'm sorry,' she said, drawing away from him. 'I should have known better, shouldn't I? And now you're as dirty as I am. And your poor mother is *still* waiting for my help.'

'Mother will manage. She always does. Both of us will wash off quite nicely, and if all you've lost is a pair of running shoes and your dignity—it could be a lot worse.'

Amber laughed shakily. 'I suppose it could. And at least I've learned about bogs.'

'Have you?' asked Kyle softly. 'I told you there was a lot you didn't know. But if you've discovered that for yourself, my dear, then the day has not been wasted.'

'Toad,' said Amber. But she was really too drained to argue.

Besides—he was right.

She started up the steep path which had been such a breeze to cover on the way down, and immediately her bare toes hit a tree-root, and she stumbled.

'Don't be an idiot,' said Kyle. 'You can't make it up there with no shoes on.'

'Of course I can. Besides, I don't have any choice.'

'Yes, you do. I'm used to carrying passengers.'

As Amber turned to gape at him, he slipped an arm quickly around her shoulders, and another beneath her knees. Before she knew what was happening he had her clasped tightly against his chest and his long legs were striding up the path.

'Hey!' cried Amber. 'Hey, wait a minute. You can't lug me all the way up there. I'm not exactly a feather-weight, you know.'

'I'm beginning to find that out,' agreed Kyle feelingly, his steps becoming noticeably less enthusiastic. 'How can anyone who looks like a feather weigh as much as a ton of bricks?'

'I *don't* weigh as much as a ton of bricks,' objected Amber. 'And, contrary to your delusions of grandeur, Kyle Maki, you are *not* Hercules and this is a very steep path.'

'So I've noticed,' replied Kyle, continuing to labour up the hill and making no attempt whatsoever to put her down.

Right, thought Amber. Play Hercules and Davy Crockett combined. *Break* your back if it suits you. See if I care.

Meanwhile, she had to admit that it was very nice to be held against his solid masculine chest and borne up the pathway without any effort on her part. If she turned her head a little she could hear his heartbeat which, as they reached the top, was becoming increasingly rapid.

'Definitely bricks,' said Kyle as he dumped her unceremoniously on her feet.

'Well, you did bring it on yourself,' Amber pointed out unrepentantly.

Kyle shook his head. 'I did, didn't I? I should have thrown you out of the car yesterday—right about where we stopped to see the Sleeping Giant. Then I could have made a fancy getaway.'

'I do wish you'd rid yourself of this obsession about throwing me off things and out of things,' grumbled Amber. 'And, anyway, your fancy getaway would probably have landed you in court.'

'Such touching faith in my driving,' murmured Kyle. 'I should have left you to be eaten by the moose.'

'You told me mooses don't bother people.'

'Whatever I told you, it certainly didn't involve "mooses".' He glanced down at her bare, muddy feet. 'You know, in spite of your opinion of my steering ability, young lady, you're going to have to trust it for the present. There's no way you can walk across the quarry without shoes.'

'You could go back to my trailer and fetch some.'

'And keep Mother waiting even longer? Nonsense.' Again he scooped her up in his arms, and again it felt disconcertingly right. He smelled nice, too, even covered in mud. But this time it was mostly downhill, and when Kyle deposited her at her door his breathing was almost steady. He let his hands linger just a second longer than was necessary on her waist.

And he didn't say a word about bricks.

'I'll just have a quick wash,' began Amber a little breathlessly.

'You'll just have a quick shower,' Kyle contradicted her.

'Yes, but there's no shower——'

'In your trailer. I know there isn't. So get some clean clothes—and some shoes—and come and join me over in the cabin. There *is* a shower in there.'

Amber eyed him doubtfully. 'Yes, but won't you be using it?'

He grinned. 'I will.'

'Then...'

The grin broadened. 'It's all right, kitten. I'm not in the habit of seducing students in the shower.'

Amber frowned. He was making her feel like a silly schoolgirl again. And he wasn't *that* much older than she was.

But he saw that he had ruffled her feelings and added placatingly, 'By the time you've collected your belongings, I'll be through. I promise. It only takes me a second to have a shower.'

Amber's frown lifted and she smiled. 'You must be Hercules and Davy Crockett *and* the Roadrunner combined,' she teased him.

'Not to mention a toad?' Kyle mocked her gently. 'I'm a very versatile fellow, aren't I? Or I have been since I met you. See you in a minute.' He put his hand briefly on her shoulder and moved off across the clearing.

Amber paused to watch him, and wondered how anyone could saunter with such speed.

A few minutes later, carrying an armful of clothing, she presented herself in the doorway of the cabin.

Kyle was standing with his back to her. It was a broad, brown and very bare back on which the moisture from the shower had not quite dried. Beneath it, a brief white towel only just covered his thighs.

Wow! thought Amber involuntarily. Golden-blond on top of golden-brown, with white to provide the contrast. What a vision. And a body... No. Uh-uh. Never mind his body. That belonged to Christina. And, anyway, she wasn't interested. If a casual roll

in the hay were all she wanted, she'd had plenty of
opportunities for those at college—and never been re-
motely tempted.

Then as Kyle, sensing she was in the room, started
to turn around, she felt a surge of something warm
and intoxicating snake up through her limbs, turning
them soft and limp. It occurred to her that it was a
pity that there wasn't much hay to roll in at Flatrock—
and was immediately angry with herself for thinking
it.

But now Kyle was facing her, and his front view
was as devastatingly seductive as his back—lean and
bronzed and rippling with animal health and vitality.
She ran her tongue over her lips as a slow smile crossed
his face and he remarked cheerfully that she looked
like an animated mudpie.

Amber felt more like a frozen mudpie, even in all
this heat, because she seemed to be having trouble
speaking, or even moving. 'I . . .' she croaked uncertainly. 'I . . .'

'You, my dear Amber, had better have your shower.'
Kyle jerked his head at the room behind him and
Amber was reminded of the time she had first noticed
him, just two days ago at the Customs office. His
head had jerked at her in just that autocratic way then.

'Yes,' she agreed, her attack of temporary rigor
mortis receding. 'Yes, I had—better have it.'

Walking quickly past him with her head averted,
she slipped into the shower. And as the cool water
slid over her body, washing away the dirt and grime
of the lake, she felt her tense antagonism towards Kyle
dissipate, and run off down the drain with the mud.

He was nice really, or he could be when she wasn't
rubbing him the wrong way. They had got off to a
bad start, of course, but she had to admit that that

had been mostly her fault. She had been thoroughly rude and condescending when he'd tried to talk to her outside the Customs building. And it was true, for all she had denied it, that she *had* regarded him as a step down the social and intellectual ladder just because he happened to drive a coach. She shook her hair hastily out of her eyes. Well, he had certainly proved her wrong there, hadn't he? No wonder he had taken her measure so quickly and set out to reduce her to size. With quite devastating success, too.

Amber tilted her head back to let the water run over her breasts, and let out a long, regretful sigh. She really had been awful. *And* she knew it. Although she had been aware for some time that she had a tendency to overplay her intelligence whenever she was around her family, that was only because her parents, and particularly her father, had an equal tendency to minimise her achievements. They thought that taking her studies seriously was a total waste of time, and that she should concentrate on the social side of college. Amber, who had the same ingrained obstinacy and persistence that had helped Harry Jones to triumph above his ordinary beginnings, was determined to show him that she could succeed on her own merits, and that she needn't depend on his money—or any man's—to set her on her path in life.

All the same, she thought ruefully, Harry's money had certainly made life easier for her than it was for some of her fellow students. But then she never tried to come the bright little brat over them. Only over her less-than-admiring parents—and, for some reason she hadn't yet figured out, over Kyle.

Kyle! Oh, hell! She had been dreaming in the shower for ages, using up all the lovely water, and that bronzed Hercules out there was undoubtedly confirming his opinion that she was a silly, thoughtless little girl—who couldn't tell sand from a bog and didn't know a thing about moose.

Damn, she was muttering to herself as she scrambled on to the bathmat and grabbed a towel. By now, at best Kyle must be convinced that she hadn't the remotest idea about time. At worst, he probably thought she didn't care that she was keeping everyone waiting.

But when Amber padded back into the living-room, all pink and glowing and beginning to heat up again much too quickly, Kyle only stared at her with a strange little smile on his face and remarked that soap and water did a lot more for her complexion than mud.

Amber didn't bother to tell him that the rosiness in her cheeks was not entirely due to the beneficial properties of soap. Thank goodness he had now discarded his towel in favour of jeans and a shirt.

'Sorry I took so long,' she mumbled, slipping into a clean pair of running shoes.

'No problem. The wait was worth the result.' He grinned. 'In the old days I'd have waited much longer.'

Amber blinked. 'You would? Why?'

'Because you'd have been in the sauna, not the shower.'

'Oh, yes, we've got one of those at home.'

'Not like the original sauna, you haven't. No electric heating in those days. You'd have sat on a bench in a log hut with one door, one window and one plugged airhole and cooked yourself in the steam from heated rocks—while you beat your beautiful body with a switch to stimulate circulation.' He smiled suggestively.

'Mmm,' murmured Amber doubtfully. 'Sounds kinky.'

The smile turned into a leer. 'And the whole family used to bathe together.'

'Definitely kinky.'

'Not at all. The old-timers believed nudity and cleanliness went together. Sex,' he added, eyeing her repressively, 'remained properly in the bedroom.'

'Just as it should be,' replied Amber, tilting her small nose up and trying to hide a smile.

'Oh, absolutely.' Kyle's blue eyes were fixed on a point above her head, but he, too, was having trouble keeping his face straight.

Then both of them gave up the effort and they exchanged grins.

'I'm sorry I laughed at you for getting stuck in the mud,' said Kyle after a while, putting an arm casually around her shoulders as he led her through the door.

Amber looked up at him and giggled. 'It's all right. I guess I did look funny.'

'Very. But I shouldn't have teased you.'

'I expect you should, really. I'd have laughed if it had been the other way around, and you'd been stuck. It's just that it didn't seem funny at the time. I was scared.'

'I know.' His fingers tightened almost imperceptibly on her arm.

She sighed. 'Besides, it wouldn't have been the other way around, would it?'

'Oh, I don't know. Not in this case, perhaps, but I have done some pretty dumb things in my day.'

Amber nearly made a cutting comment, thought better of it just in time, and ended up biting her tongue. A moment later Kyle was pushing her ahead

of him through the door of the gift shop and Helvi
was bustling towards them.

'Kyle, what have you been up to?' she demanded.
'I told you to give Amber a quick tour of the mine
and then bring her straight over here.'

'It was my fault,' began Kyle and Amber in unison.

Helvi stared from one to the other of them and
shook her head. 'I don't believe it,' she muttered.

'No, it really was my fault,' insisted Amber. She
explained about sleeping in, and getting stuck in the
muck, and the moose, and then having to shower.

By the time she had finished, Helvi was leaning
against a glass shelf displaying amethyst bookends,
and her well-upholstered body was quivering with un-
restrained laughter.

'Never mind, never mind,' she chuckled at last,
wiping away the tears which were still streaming down
her face. 'You've given me the best laugh I've had in
a long time. And you've surely learned something
about our lakes.' She pulled at the blue overall she
was wearing and became all business again. 'Kyle, you
go and see if your father and Erik need any help today.
I'm going to show Amber how to run the shop.'

'Whatever you say, Mother,' said Kyle with suspicious docility, as he made his way to the door.

'Hmm,' grunted Helvi at his retreating back.
'That'll be the day you do what anyone says—unless
it's what you want to do yourself.'

On the step Kyle paused to say piously, 'Misjudged
again. Don't believe a word of it, kitten.'

'You'd better believe it,' grumbled Helvi, as she led
Amber towards a showcase by the wall. 'That one will
be the death of his father if he keeps it up.'

'Umm—keeps what up?' asked Amber, not sure whether she ought to ask, but very curious just the same.

'This coach-driving business. It's making my Reijo crazy.' Helvi put her hands on her hips and added decisively, 'I'm going to have words with both those men of mine. They're as stubborn as a couple of mules, and I'm not having Kyle's visit spoiled by any such foolishness.'

Amber had no doubt that if Helvi had her mind set on peace in her household, she would get it. But there was one thing she still didn't understand.

'Umm, yes,' she murmured diffidently. 'But, I mean—well, I know Mr Maki doesn't like what Kyle is doing...but is he really trained to do anything else?'

In the act of lifting a glass lid, Helvi paused to stare at her helper, her round face a mask of surprise. 'You mean he didn't tell you?'

'No-o. Tell me what?'

'That he gave up a successful career with the English department at the University of Toronto—to drive a *coach*.'

'Oh-h,' said Amber on a long drawn-out breath. 'Oh, no. Oh, dear. That explains it.'

And it did explain it. It explained a lot of things. Reijo's resentment, Kyle's knowledge of very unmodern poetry—and, above all, his half-amused contempt for the snooty little college girl who had thought he couldn't know anything much because he drove a coach.

'Oh, dear,' she repeated.

'Yes,' said Helvi briefly. And Amber knew the subject of Kyle's chosen profession was closed.

Helvi banged the lid against the wall with a snap and began to tell Amber about the glowing purple jewellery nested on velvet cushions in the case. Beautiful dark purple rings in silver settings, pendants, necklaces and earrings in shades of mauve and violet. Some of them were set in clusters with other stones. All of them reflected the light shining through the window, and patterns of purple fire danced on the wall behind them as Helvi brought out piece after sparkling piece to show to Amber.

'These are our more expensive items,' she explained, 'so we keep the cases locked. But over here we have jewellery to suit any purse.' She indicated a long counter in the centre of the room, and Amber saw trays of twinkling gems set out in small white boxes. Other cases and shelves contained amethyst pen sets, clocks, crystal balls, vases and figurines in a variety of purple shapes and sizes. On a table near the cash register was a display of rocks streaked with the precious colour. Amber nodded, fascinated, as Helvi showed her how to wash the rocks, set out the displays and, of course, operate the cash register.

Soon the party of Minnesota choristers she had seen earlier erupted into the shop, and Amber was able to gain experience under Helvi's watchful eye as she rang up a string of purchases.

By the end of the day she even felt as though she knew what she was doing, and by then also she knew that, whatever her father thought, her decision to take a job this summer had been the right one for her.

In the evening, feeling tired but satisfied, she again had supper with the Makis, and although both Helvi and Reijo made an effort to entertain her Kyle was unusually silent, and she sensed that the hard feelings between him and his father had not in any way abated.

Amber was just getting undressed that night when there was a peremptory knock on her door.

'Open up!' shouted Kyle.

Amber opened up, and he was standing in the moonlight, looking more Greek-godlike than ever and holding a small travel alarm clock in his hand. 'Here,' he said, taking her wrist and placing the clock in her upturned palm. 'And don't forget to use it. If I have to wake you again you won't like it.'

Amber, remembering his threats of the morning, was inclined to agree that she wouldn't.

'Thanks,' she said shortly. 'Don't worry, I won't forget.'

He nodded, stared at her with a faintly puzzled expression on his face and started to lean towards her. For a moment she thought he was going to kiss her, then he seemed to recollect himself, closed his eyes briefly, and straightened.

'Goodnight,' he said brusquely.

Amber whispered goodnight to his tall silhouette as it disappeared into the darkness. Then she closed the door, leaned against it and sighed.

She did not see Kyle again until the evening of her fourth day at Flatrock. She supposed he must have been away visiting friends, but now he strolled into the gift shop just as she was closing up, and he had the man he had called Erik in tow.

'You look heated,' he remarked sympathetically as Amber began ringing off the cash. 'Job getting you down?'

'No, of course not.' She pushed at a lock of copper hair which had fallen over her eyes. 'But it is hot, isn't it? I've been boiled ever since I opened up. And just to make sure I didn't get a chance to cool down, I've had at least ten tour groups in today.'

'Don't I know it,' muttered the dark-haired Erik with feeling.

Kyle smiled. 'Amber, I don't think you've been formally introduced to Erik. He's a hard man to catch up with.'

'No, I'm not,' said Erik gloomily. 'You just can't find me behind all those predatory tourists.'

'Not predatory, Erik. Merely enthusiastic.' Kyle turned to Amber. 'Erik prefers playing with dynamite and drills,' he told her. 'He has an unfortunate passion for noise.'

'That last tour group was pretty noisy,' agreed Amber, 'but I guess they weren't positively explosive.'

'Depends what you mean by explosive,' muttered Erik. 'They nearly made *me* explode.'

Amber pulled the cover over the cash register, picked up the green sweater which, due to a moment of wishful thinking, she had brought in with her that morning, and started to turn off the lights.

'Just a minute,' said Kyle, catching her arm as she made her way to the door. 'I have a proposition for you. Or rather Erik has. He says you're too young to be marooned out here in the bush——'

'But I *like* it here.'

'And that as he and Rosie are going into town for dinner,' Kyle continued, ignoring the interruption, 'you might like to make up a foursome and go in with them as well.'

Amber's grey-green eyes were sceptical. 'Is that a backhanded invitation to dinner?' she asked caustically. 'Because if it is——'

Kyle leaned against the door-jamb, so that she couldn't get past him. 'On the contrary,' he replied coolly. 'All quite up front and above-board. Will you have dinner with me—and with Erik and Rose—tonight in Thunder Bay? There. Is that better?'

Amber's heart gave an annoying lurch, and she wished she didn't want to say 'yes'. He looked very male, leaning there in a blue shirt that did nothing to conceal the outline of his chest, and with those tight jeans practically embracing his well-formed thighs ...

'No,' she said quickly.

Kyle sighed. 'What have I done now?'

'Nothing, but you don't really want to take me out for dinner.'

He sighed again, this time with impatience, and the warm voice became slightly bored. 'Keep it up and I won't want to, kitten. But, believe me, I wouldn't have asked you unless I approved of the idea.'

For some reason Amber did believe him. But just as she had never been able to resist getting to the bottom of things, she had never known when to let a subject drop.

'But it wasn't *your* idea, was it?' she persisted. 'And I'm sure Erik was only being kind.'

'Of course he was being kind!' snapped Kyle, with difficulty conquering an urge to take her by the shoulders and shake her. 'Do you have some objection to kindness, Amber? And no, you argumentative little witch, it *wasn't* my idea in the first place, but that doesn't mean I don't think it's a good one.'

'Oh. Do you mean you actually *want* to take me into town?'

'Lord preserve me from women who don't use the ears they were born with,' groaned Kyle, raising his eyes to the rafters. 'No, Miss Amber Jones. Of course I don't want to take you into town. That's obviously why I asked you.'

Behind her, Amber heard Erik give a snort of amusement. 'Well, there's no need to be sarcastic,' she said huffily.

'Yes, there is. Sarcasm is the fine line between you and very physical violence, young lady. I've had about all I'm going to take from you.'

Amber stared at him. On principle she didn't approve of violence. But there was something so utterly seductive about the lean, supple body lounging in the doorway glaring at her that for a moment—a very *brief* moment—she felt something inside her rise eagerly to meet his challenge, and she wished he would lay his hands on her—just so that she could fight him back. Then sanity returned and she replied mildly, 'In that case, thank you. Yes, I'd love to have dinner with you and Erik and Rosie.'

Kyle groaned again and shook his head in frustration. 'All that, just to get a simple "yes". Are you always so difficult to get along with, kitten?'

Amber saw that in spite of himself he was half amused, and she felt a surprising emotion sweep over her that had nothing to do with his physical presence, and more to do with—what? Affection, almost. He really was being thoughtful, and so far all she had done was give him a bad time.

'What would you like me to wear?' she asked quickly, wanting to be co-operative now and asking the first thing that came to mind.

'Something sexy,' said Erik hopefully.

'You're a married man, my friend.' Kyle shook his head reprovingly. 'Amber, you'd better wear something respectable, or you'll be leading Erik astray.'

'I'm always respectable,' replied Amber demurely.

'Really? How disappointing.'

Amber, glancing at him sharply, saw that he was smiling again, and knew a stab of disappointment herself. There just wasn't any point in thinking Kyle would take her seriously. He had made up his mind that she was a tiresome, if sometimes amusing, little girl, and for the remainder of his stay he would continue to treat her kindly, she was sure. At the back of her mind she was aware that it was just that casual kindness which aroused all the worst contrary instincts of her nature. No wonder it would never even occur to him to think of her as a woman.

But that was where Amber was wrong.

Kyle called out that he would pick her up at seven, and began to make his way back to the trailer that he was living in because Helvi had turned his old bedroom into a store-room for stock from the shop. And as he strolled across the car park it very definitely occurred to him, with some alarm, that in spite of Amber's youth and seeming innocence it was impossible *not* to think of her as a woman. And he didn't want to think of her that way in the least.

She was his parents' employee and in their care. Not only that, she was young, the same age as many of the students he had taught, and he had always been particularly careful never to take advantage of his position of authority in those days. Not that he hadn't had the opportunity, he mused, half regretfully. Some of the lures that had been cast at him by nubile young women had been very enticing. Very enticing indeed. And not all his colleagues had shared his scruples, either. He remembered that there had been quite a scandal only the year before last...

No. It just wasn't worth it. He smiled ruefully to himself. Was he becoming a lecherous old fool already—at the ripe old age of thirty-four? Apparently he was, and of course it couldn't go on. He stared moodily at a crow which had settled on top of the cabin. It wasn't going to be easy to forget how soft and warm Amber's mud-caked body had been as he'd carried her up from the lake—or the way her cheek had nestled into his chest . . .

Hell. He had avoided her for the past few days, but when Erik had suggested this outing it had seemed only fair to give her a chance to get out and have some fun. Now he was beginning to wonder if it had been such a good idea, after all. He shoved his hands into his pockets, stirred a chunk of grey stone absently with his foot, and began to whistle tunelessly through his teeth.

Perhaps Amber, with all her objections and arguments, had been right in the first place. With a quick movement of his hand, he pulled open the door of his trailer, remembering her face as she had glared up at him, full of doubt and belligerence.

Then he smiled crookedly, shrugged his shoulders and began opening and shutting drawers much too forcefully and for no particular reason.

Amber stared at herself in the skinny mirror on the back of her bathroom door. Erik had said sexy, Kyle respectable, and she had tried to comply with both their requests. Now, smoothing her hands critically over her hips and turning to inspect her side-view, she wasn't at all sure that she had succeeded.

She was wearing a red dress which only just missed being blazing scarlet. With her copper hair it made her look very—well, *red*. There was no other way to describe it. Her mother had always said that she couldn't wear red, but her mother hadn't been with her in Buffalo—and she had fallen in love with the low-backed halter-neck dress that flared out over her hips and swirled around her in soft folds as she moved. Aunt Janet had said she looked lovely in it. But then

Mother said Aunt Janet had no taste... Oh, dear. Maybe it *was* too much. Maybe she ought to change.

But a horn hooted noisily outside. Amber ignored it, and almost immediately a loud knock sounded on her door. Right. This was it, then. No time to change even if she wanted to.

With a last quick check of her hair and make-up, Amber fixed a confident smile on her face and went out to meet Kyle in the sunlight.

'You look like a beautiful firefly,' he said appreciatively as his eyes ran over her figure—and Amber hoped that her pleasure at his praise wasn't glowing in her face to match the dress.

'Thank you,' she said politely. 'Do you like it?'

'What man wouldn't? But I thought I told you *respectable*, Amber Jones.'

Her eyes flew to his face, then anxiously to the front of her dress. 'What? I thought—is something wrong with it? Have I ripped somewhere?'

'Unfortunately, no. You're not showing anything you shouldn't be.' He grinned wickedly. 'You do look very sexy, though. Erik will be delighted.'

Amber wasn't particularly interested in delighting Erik, but, now that Kyle mentioned him, where *was* the instigator of this expedition? They had reached the car and Kyle was opening the passenger door, but there was certainly no sign of the other couple.

'Where are Erik and Rose?' she asked him. 'Are we picking them up on the way?'

'No, we're meeting them in Thunder Bay. They went in early so that Rosie could shop, and they're spending the night with her parents. So we had to bring separate cars,' he explained offhandedly.

Too offhandedly, decided Amber. His eyes were running lazily over her figure again, and the look in

their sensuous blue depths was altogether seductive—
as she had been altogether mistaken. There could be
no possible doubt that Kyle had noticed that she was
a woman.

Her stomach gave a lurch that was half hopeful and
half fearful. She was going to be alone with this
frighteningly attractive man all the way in to Thunder
Bay—and, if she read his expression correctly, she
would be lucky if they got there.

CHAPTER FIVE

AMBER need not have worried—except perhaps about Kyle's habitual impatience to get where he was going. He drove with his usual skill, and at breakneck speed, down the highway into town, and there was no question of stopping for seduction or any other purpose. Provided, of course, that they survived other equally uninhibited drivers and avoided the attentions of a vigilant highway patrol. Fleetingly, it occurred to Amber that it was just as well that he didn't drive his coach the same way he drove the Flatrock transportation.

Kyle was silent for the better part of the journey, and, although he steered most of the time with only one hand on the wheel, he made no attempt to touch her. In fact, he didn't look at her at all, keeping his eyes strictly on the curving snake of a road.

Amber wasn't sure whether to be relieved or disappointed, but as they arrived on the outskirts of the city and drove past the neat suburban houses along Hodder Avenue she realised that, despite Kyle's aloofness, she was unlikely to be offered a better opportunity than this to satisfy her curiosity about his startling change in career. She had seen so little of him lately that she hadn't had a chance to question him about Helvi's surprising revelation.

'What made you give up the university?' she asked abruptly, as they turned a corner and swept past the Current River Dam. 'I mean, I had no idea when I first met you——'

'I know. And I don't see why it makes a difference. For your information, coach-drivers don't get along with nothing more going for them than a commercial driving licence and the space between their ears.'

Amber sighed. He sounded cold and superior again, and she didn't want the evening to be spoiled. 'No, of course they don't,' she began, 'and of course it makes no difference——'

'They need the patience of Job,' he continued as if he hadn't heard her, 'the understanding of a psychologist, the muscles of Atlas—and the skill of a racing-car driver, when it comes to negotiating some of the maniacs who are let loose on our roads.' He honked his horn and swerved past a Volkswagen and two campers which were sedately observing the speed limit.

Amber stifled a laugh and glanced over at him quickly, but his profile was definitely hawklike at the moment and she swallowed the caustic remark which had sprung to her lips.

Oh, dear. Kyle was going to be difficult this evening. First he had treated her as if she were a child to be amused for a few hours, then he had turned all predatory and male, and now he seemed to have become the cold, disapproving instructor in 'proper' values again. Thank goodness Erik and Rosie would be around for most of the evening.

'I'm sure you're right about driving a coach,' she said placatingly. 'It must present a great many—challenges.' This was certainly not the time to press for further details about Kyle's past.

I'm learning, she thought, as they pulled up in front of a hotel not far from the water. Even earlier today I would probably have kept on questioning. But not tonight. Tonight I want peace and harmony. *And*, she added to herself as she watched his firm hands on the wheel and admired the attractive figure he made in his light grey summer suit, I think I also want Kyle.

She froze with her hand on the handle of the door. What was she *thinking*? Was she crazy? It was true he was mouth-watering to look at, and often he was kind and amusing, but he was also irritating and self-righteous—and he obviously didn't want her. Her fingers tightened on the handle. That wasn't quite true, was it? Kyle probably did want her, as much as she wanted him. But, of course, that was all there was to it. Want. Lust. Amber sighed. She had never been thoroughly in lust before, and she had to admit that it felt exceptionally nice. Exciting, too. But did she want that? Brief excitement, and the satisfaction of a passion which would inevitably lead to grief and heartbreak in the future? No, on the whole she didn't think she did. But she would have to consider it later.

Much later, she realised, because now Kyle was pulling open the door which still had her hand attached to the handle—and he was bending down to help her out of the car.

'Thank you,' she said quickly as he hauled her up beside him. Then her breath caught somewhere in her throat, because he wasn't moving away from her and his arm was circling purposefully around her waist.

Kyle felt her body stiffen, and smiled slightly. 'It's all right,' he said softly. 'I'm not going any further.'

Still with his arm around her, he drew her across the car park to the big glass doors of the hotel. And now Amber *knew* that her face matched her hair and dress, because heat was welling up in her like a furnace and she had no idea whether it was his touch that was causing this reaction, or embarrassment that he had so easily guessed her thoughts.

She was still desperately trying to dampen the flames, both external and internal, when Kyle led her into the dining-room and they were escorted to a table by the window where Erik and Rosie were already sipping their drinks.

'Oh, ho,' said Erik, his dark eyes bright with speculation. 'I see you took my advice on what to wear, Amber. And from the colour of your face, I think it's had the desired effect.'

'What are you talking about?' demanded Amber, feeling sure that the colour in question had just deepened to fuchsia fire.

'Well, it looks to me as if my fast-working friend, Kyle here, has been making indecent suggestions.'

'Certainly not,' said Kyle virtuously, pulling out a chair for Amber and nodding at her to sit down. 'You know me better than that.'

'I know you all too well, my friend,' replied Erik with a grin. He put his head on one side and pretended to consider the matter carefully. 'All right, then, if you're going to uphold decency and morality for a change—that leaves the field clear for me, doesn't it? That dress of Amber's really shouldn't be allowed to go to waste.'

'Hold it, buster,' chipped in the perky little blonde seated beside him. 'You're already spoken for. Remember? And Amber belongs to Kyle.'

'Heaven forbid,' muttered Kyle under his breath as he lowered himself on to the remaining vacant chair.

'Thanks,' Amber muttered back, 'and you're not any prize yourself.'

Rose giggled. 'Oh-oh. Are we having a lovers' spat? I'm Rose, by the way, Amber, since neither of these charming gentlemen seems inclined to introduce us.'

'You didn't give us the chance, did you?' said Erik aggrievedly.

'Amber, meet Rose, Erik's sweet and reticent helpmate,' murmured Kyle, with a provocative smile at Erik's wife which made Amber suspect that these two had been affectionate sparring partners for years.

'Hello, Rose,' smiled Amber.

'And, Rose dear, just to set the record straight,' added Kyle in a tone which had a definite edge to it, 'Amber and I are *not* having a lovers' spat——'

'No,' agreed Amber quickly, making sure he didn't get the chance to say it first. 'We're not. Because we're not lovers. And we're not likely to be, either.'

'Precisely,' said Kyle. His eyes slanted at her enigmatically, and the edge was more cutting than ever.

Amber glared at him. He really was being impossible this evening. She hadn't *asked* him to take her out, and yet he was behaving like a boy who had had his plans to go fishing ruined because his mother had insisted he entertain a whiny visiting child. What Kyle needed, she decided, was a good swift kick in the pants. And given much more provocation, that's exactly what he'd get.

This conclusion filled her with considerable satisfaction, until it occurred to her that Kyle was the sort of man who would take equal satisfaction in kicking back. She heaved a small, regretful sigh. Obviously the best thing to do was ignore him—as much as she humanly could. The trouble was, he was also the sort of man whom it was extremely hard to ignore. There was rather a lot of him for one thing.

Luckily Erik and Rose seemed determined to make the evening a success, and Amber was delighted to discover that she felt an immediate affinity with the bright and outspoken Rose, who told her that she ran a small grocery shop about five miles up the highway from the mine. Erik, too, was full of fun and laughter as he pointed out the view of Lake Superior from the window and began to tell Amber the legend of the Giant.

'She's already heard it,' said Kyle, seeming drawn into the conversation against his will.

'Yes,' agreed Amber, 'but I don't mind hearing it again.'

He raised his eyebrows. 'Really? If you're worrying about Erik's feelings getting hurt—don't. He hasn't got any.'

'Yes, he has,' objected Rose. 'What you really mean is *you* don't like being bored.'

'True. You know me too well, don't you, Rosie?'

'She'd better *not* know you too well,' snorted Erik.

'Ah. He's getting suspicious, Rosie love. We'll have to watch our step.' Kyle flashed a wolfish grin at Erik's pretty wife.

'If you're trying to incite Erik to violence, it won't work,' Rose told him flatly. 'My husband is never distracted from his food.'

'Pity. Then I'll have to incite Amber instead.'

'Oh, no, you won't. I'm a pacifist,' said Amber firmly.

Kyle lifted a lock of her hair. 'You can't be. Not with hair like this.' His lips curved in a possessive, intimate smile.

'That has nothing to do with it,' scoffed Amber, tossing her head and twisting the lock from his grasp. She picked up her fork and prodded purposefully at her plate.

But the thaw had set in, and for the remainder of the meal Kyle became the amusing, if thoroughly confusing man she had come to know, instead of the acid-tongued toad.

The food was good, the company was good and the conversation surprisingly easy. When Rose announced that she and Erik must go, because it was already ten o'clock and her parents were early risers, Amber was amazed and a little deflated to find that the evening had passed so quickly.

Kyle said nothing as he helped her back into the car, and she found that she didn't have much to say herself until she realised that they were not returning the way they had come, but were driving uphill, along a street called Red River Road. A few minutes later they turned left, and at that point Amber let out a yelp and said, 'Hey, you're going the wrong way.'

'No, I'm not.'

'Look,' said Amber patiently, 'I may be pretty dense about mud-flats and moose, but I have a very good sense of direction. Believe me, this is not the way we came.'

Kyle gave her an irritating little smile, replied that there was nothing wrong with his sense of direction either, and swerved to a stop at a point high above the city.

'Hillcrest Park,' he announced, waving at dimly lit gardens.

Amber stared in surprise. She hadn't expected anything like this. Far below them the lights of Thunder Bay glimmered in the warm summer air. In the distance the blackness of Lake Superior was broken here and there by the lamps of shipping, and by one bright beam which stood out among the rest and which Kyle told her was the Welcome Island Lighthouse.

'How lovely,' she breathed. 'Thank you for showing me.' She smiled a little self-consciously. 'You did know where you were going, after all.'

'I always do. Well, almost always,' he amended after a brief pause.

'In that case, where are you going now?' asked Amber, because Kyle was opening the door and stepping out into the night.

'Come and join me, and you'll find out.'

'Why? I don't see——'

'You will.' He reached inside, caught her by the wrists and pulled her, still resisting, up beside him. She wasn't quite sure why it was necessary to resist, but somehow it seemed important.

'Why...?' she began again, feeling a rush of warmth as he placed his hands on her shoulders and turned her around to face him.

'Because I've been fighting my instincts all evening. And now I'm going to let them have their way.'

'What...?' Amber frowned, puzzled, nervous and—yes, she had to admit it—alive with anticipation.

'I want to kiss you, Amber. And I'm damned if we're going to do it coiled around the steering-wheel of a car like a couple of adolescents with the itch.'

'But——'

'Don't give me any buts, kitten.' His hands were moving down her back now, and his mouth was very close to hers. Her body had gone rigid, her senses were reeling and her arms were pressed tightly to her sides. And she couldn't have said 'but' if she had tried.

Only she didn't try.

Slowly, breathtakingly slowly, Kyle's mouth descended over hers, and those lips which she had once thought too thin to be sensual were proving with devastating efficiency exactly how wrong she had been.

She still couldn't move, but there was a feeling in her chest which was spreading throughout her body, something glowing, a sort of melting, and as Kyle's lips moved to the hollow of her throat, and then behind her ear, she knew with a surge of desire that if she didn't respond to his kiss she would explode.

Gradually her limbs relaxed. Kyle, feeling it, moved his arms around her waist and pulled her hard against him. Her own arms crept around his neck, and then her fingers were twined in the golden helmet of his hair which she had always longed to touch. She turned her mouth to meet his again, and this time his kiss was harder, more insistent, and she felt his tongue ease between her teeth, tantalising her, and arousing sensations and desires that were more powerful and more shattering than anything she had ever felt before. Or dreamed of.

As her hands explored the muscles of his back and moved wonderingly across the silky fabric of his shirt, she let out a little gasp.

And Kyle, hearing her, returned to earth and gently held her away.

'Amber,' he said softly. 'Kitten...'

Amber shook her head, and saw stars tumble in front of her eyes—until she realised that they were in the sky above her, and really not moving at all.

'Kyle?' she whispered.

She couldn't quite see the colour of his eyes in the dim lighting of the garden, but there was something in the way he was standing, silhouetted against the city, that made her uneasy. He seemed unnaturally tall, with his legs apart and his magnificent body so still that he looked like the statue of some mythical and primitive god. But it was a very cold statue, wary and withdrawn now, not the kind that in ancient legends conveniently sprang to life.

'Kyle?' she said again, louder this time.

Instead of answering, he turned away from her and stared out over the darkness of the lake.

'What *is* it?' she pleaded, a note almost of desperation in her voice.

At that he turned towards her, lifted his hand as if to touch her cheek, then dropped it again and took a deliberate step away.

'I'm sorry, Amber,' he said tonelessly. 'I had no right to do that. I apologise.'

'You don't have to apologise. It—I—liked it...' The words were ridiculously inadequate, but at least they were the truth.

'I know. That's even more reason for me to apologise.'

'I don't understand...'

'I was afraid you wouldn't. Listen, Amber, just forget it ever happened. You don't have to understand. I was overcome with a fit of—moonlight and midsummer madness, I suppose.' He ran his hand through his hair, making Amber want to touch it again, to push her fingers through the fair, shining waves.

But Kyle was telling her that that was out of the question.

'I can't make you any promises, Amber. It was irresponsible and unfair of me to take advantage, but you looked so incredibly sweet and sexy that I wanted to kiss you the moment you stepped out of that trailer. I'm a man like any other man, I'm afraid, and in the end I couldn't fight it any more.'

So that was why he had been so impossible and infuriating all evening. And it wasn't very flattering to be regarded as something to fight off like a mosquito. But he wasn't a man like other men. He was Kyle. And he was more seductive and disturbing and—desirable than any other man she had ever met. Amber felt the first stirrings of indignation. Why was he telling her that he couldn't make any promises? She hadn't asked for any, had she? He was behaving almost as if he thought she would expect him to *marry* her, just because he had kissed her. Once. Of all the *ridiculous* ideas.

'It was only a kiss,' she said coldly, suddenly wanting to hurt him. 'I honestly don't see what all the fuss is about.'

'Only a——' He stopped, the angry exclamation dying on his lips. 'Yes. Well, as long as that's quite clear——'

'Why shouldn't it be? Do you really think you're so irresistible that I'm going to be reduced to a quivering jelly just because you happened to touch me?'

She had, of course, been reduced to precisely that. A quivering jelly described her condition very well. But she wasn't going to let him know it. Arrogant toad that he was.

'No,' he was saying now, his voice low, controlled and completely without emotion. 'No, Amber, my dear, I don't think you're a quivering jelly. Far from it. Although you quivered very nicely in my arms. However, as you say, it was only a kiss. So let's forget it.'

'Yes, *let's*!' said Amber through clenched teeth. She watched him stride swiftly to the car, sweep open the door and gesture at her peremptorily to get in. How *dared* he make fun of her because her body had responded to his touch?

With her head in the air and the red dress swirling around her hips, she stepped across the garden and eased herself on to the seat.

Kyle slammed the door, and with a quick, indrawn breath swung himself down beside her.

Amber closed her eyes. Kyle was a reckless enough driver at the best of times. In the mood he was in now he would probably be suicidal.

She kept her eyes closed, and her mouth tightly shut, all the way back to Flatrock. When she opened them again, the car had stopped and they were, miraculously, safe in the car park at the mine.

Kyle opened the door for her without speaking and walked beside her to her trailer. As she touched the handle of the door, she hesitated. He was still beside her, motionless, but making no move to take her in his arms. What *was* the matter with him? Why didn't he either go away and leave her to forget his kiss, as he had said she must, or else give up his statue act and kiss her again—and again?

She turned her head to stare up at him, her hair just brushing his arm. Even in the moonlight she could see that his eyes were hooded and unreadable. His head was bent slightly towards her and his fists were curled tightly at his sides.

Tentatively Amber reached out a hand to his face, saw him stiffen, and withdrew it. 'Goodnight, Kyle,' she said dully, wondering at her extraordinary sense of loss. 'Thank you for the evening. I enjoyed it.' Utterly banal words to describe an evening which had turned her world upside down, but they were the best she could manage.

He moved then. 'Goodnight, Amber. I—Goodnight.' Abruptly he turned on his heel and vanished into the darkness.

Amber closed her eyes, dashed away a tear which was skimming down her cheek and slammed the door of the trailer emphatically behind her.

Toad! she thought furiously. Unspeakable toad. Angrily she tugged at the red dress and pulled it off with such force that a seam ripped. And *that* was his fault, too.

It was not until she had flung a pale yellow night-dress over her head, thumped on to the narrow bed and pulled the covers up over her ears that it occurred to her that, apart from Kyle's strange silence in the car on the way in, it had been a perfectly pleasant evening until he had kissed her. *That* was when her world had overturned. But really his kiss had only been a natural culmination of earlier hours spent together. So why was she hurt and angry?

Amber pushed the covers down again and stared at the small rectangle of the window. That was the crux of the problem, wasn't it? She was not angry with him for kissing her, that was certain. In fact, now that she was attempting to face the matter squarely, it seemed that mostly she was angry because he wouldn't kiss her again—and had told her to forget that it had ever happened.

She stirred restlessly, all of a sudden feeling much too warm. So what did it all mean? *Not* that she was in love with him, because she couldn't be. Love wasn't something that had happened to her before, and she didn't expect it to until she was at least thirty and ready to settle down. She had always been quite clear in her mind about that, in spite of her father's determined efforts to attach her to thé 'right' young man. Anyway, the right young man certainly *wasn't* Kyle. He might be an extraordinarily attractive man, but that didn't make him right.

No, she thought, flinging the covers back and sitting up. No, he wasn't right. He was just as sexy as hell and she was having a delayed attack of hormones. Which obviously wouldn't last, so there was nothing to worry about, was there?

She had just reached this comforting conclusion and was about to lie down again when a movement outside the window caught her eye. Cautiously, she pushed back the thin curtain.

On the other side of the clearing a tall figure loomed in the moonlight. She saw a faint gleam of pale hair as his head jerked upwards at the sky. Then he thrust his hands into his pockets and moved off into the night.

So Kyle couldn't sleep, either.

She wondered if he too was remembering the kiss he had told her she must forget...

Kyle was not there the following evening when Amber appeared as usual in the cabin to share the family's meal.

'He's eating with Erik and Rosie,' explained Helvi, with her eyes fixed firmly on the table.

She's embarrassed, thought Amber. Which probably means he was asked to invite me too, but wouldn't do it.

Reijo scowled and muttered something under his breath about that boy being a thoughtless brat.

'He's not a boy any more, you know,' murmured Helvi gently. She sighed. 'Although sometimes I have trouble remembering that myself.'

No, agreed Amber silently. He's not a boy, and he's not my idea of a brat, either. Just a selfish toad.

The next day was again very busy at the shop, and for that Amber was thankful. She didn't want time

to think, because although there was no sign of Kyle
his presence always seemed to be lurking just around
the corner, and she found the prospect of running into
him unexpectedly disconcerting. *And* annoying, she
fumed, irritated with herself for letting him put her
at this ridiculous disadvantage.

That evening, when she walked into the cabin and
saw Kyle's long legs stretched out under the table, with
his face conveniently hidden behind a newspaper, she
felt such a jolt run through her that she thought for
a moment she had stepped on an exposed electric cord.
But she hadn't stepped on anything except Helvi's
bright woven rug. Something of her feeling must have
communicated itself to Kyle, because he lowered the
paper and looked up. Blue eyes met green ones, and
again Amber felt that convulsive electric jolt.

'Good evening, Amber.' He smiled thinly, and
Amber remembered just how sensual those unusual
lips could be.

'Good evening,' she replied primly, fighting a mild
urge to blush and a much stronger one to pick up the
nearest object—in this case a particularly striking
chunk of amethyst moulded in the shape of a fish—
and hurl it at his supercilious head.

'Don't do it,' he warned, accurately divining the
direction of her thoughts. The smile was curling up
at the corners now, and Amber felt a small sense of
triumph because, in spite of his efforts to seem indifferent and aloof, he was showing that she could
still make him smile.

She smiled back. 'I won't, as long as you keep that
disagreeable expression off your face.'

Kyle raised his eyebrows deliberately. 'I'm never
disagreeable,' he replied with overplayed dignity. But

behind the careful words Amber heard an undertone of the amusement he could barely conceal.

Supper was a much more comfortable meal tonight. Helvi had apparently made good her threat to 'talk to' her obstinate men. Kyle was casual and affectionate with his father, discussing the business of the mine with genuine warmth and interest. And Reijo had evidently decided to call a temporary truce in his war of wills with his son—a war which he had no hope of winning, as surely he had to know. Helvi smiled her relief that family peace had been restored, at least temporarily, and the smile expanded complacently when she saw that her son was behaving with gentlemanly decorum towards Amber.

The only sour note occurred while they were drinking Helvi's potent coffee and she, with a kindly beam at Amber and a maternally coercive one at Kyle, suggested that he might like to take Amber out tomorrow to show her around the district.

'Can't keep her cooped up here all summer, can we?' she said, not expecting an answer. 'And Reijo doesn't need my help tomorrow, so I can handle the shop.'

'Not possible, I'm afraid,' said Kyle with a steely note in his voice. 'I've already made plans for tomorrow.'

'What *plans*?' Helvi started to scoff. Then, seeing the way Kyle's face had hardened into an expressionless mask, she stopped, shrugged and said, almost irritably for her, that of course she wouldn't dream of interfering with his plans.

'It's quite all right, I *love* working in the shop,' said Amber with exaggerated enthusiasm, thinking that if Helvi ever did dream of interfering with Kyle's plans it wouldn't do her a whole lot of good. She wondered what it had been like raising Kyle to manhood. Not what the average mother leaving hospital with her newborn pride and joy would be likely to put on her wish list, she decided. Still, he must have been a challenge. She smiled grimly to herself. A challenge all right, but one most mothers could easily live without.

Helvi, as Amber might have known, was not one to see her plans derailed, and the next day when she arrived at the shop she found Rose waiting outside for her in a battered old pick-up truck.

'Mrs Maki has bribed my neighbour to run the store for me today,' she explained with a conspiratorial grin. 'And I've been detailed to give you a tour of the district because Kyle isn't able to do it.'

'Oh,' said Amber. 'Oh, dear. I mean . . .'

'Oh, it's all right,' said Rose breezily. 'I'm delighted. Listen, if I take you out to Kakabeka to see the Falls, that should keep Mrs M. happy—and then we can go into Thunder Bay and shop. Is that all right with you?'

'Of course it is,' laughed Amber, 'although if I do any more shopping I'll never be able to shut my suitcases again.' This proved an unfortunate train of thought, because it reminded her of Kyle swinging her bags so easily across the pavement in Toronto—and she really didn't want to think about Kyle today.

'Let's go,' she grinned, jumping up beside Rose, and waving to Helvi who was smiling smugly from behind the long window of the shop.

As Rose had planned, they drove first to Kakabeka to see the place where the Kaministiqua River stormed down the rockface in a cascade of such stunning natural grandeur that for a while Amber was speechless.

'It's—incredible,' she said at last, gazing at the foaming rainbow in which the brown of the river-bed blended with sunlight and the whiteness of the water to create its own thundering magic.

'Different from Winnipeg, eh?' said Rose with a touch of pride.

Amber came down to earth and laughed. 'Winnipeg has its charms, but it's a bit too flat for falls.'

'Right,' said Rose briskly. 'And as we've now paid tribute to Helvi Maki's idea of sightseeing, let's head for the hills—i.e. the shops,' she added hastily, seeing Amber's startled expression.

Three-quarters of an hour later they were seated in a restaurant in a large shopping mall in Fort William while Rose drank coffee and drew up lists of 'things to buy'. Amber drank tea and watched her as they waited for their lunch. When she saw that Rose had finished what was obviously a pleasurable task, she ran her fingers thoughtfully around the rim of her cup and said slowly, 'Rose...?'

'Mmm?' Rose's attention was still riveted on her list.

'Rose, you've known Kyle a long time, haven't you?'

'Uh-huh. Since we were all kids. Why?'

'I just wondered—I know it's not really my business, but sometimes there's such an atmosphere at the mine because Mr Maki resents Kyle driving a coach that—Rose, why *did* Kyle give up the university?'

'Ah,' said Rose, her attention finally diverted from the list. 'They didn't tell you, then?'

'No. Nobody told me anything. I suppose there's no reason why they should.'

'No,' agreed Rose, serious now. 'I suppose there isn't. Still, you're bound to wonder, and really it's no big secret. I suppose they just don't like talking about it. Understandable, I guess.'

'Talking about *what*?' asked Amber, her curiosity, never far from the surface, now almost at boiling-point.

Rose cleared her throat. 'Well, you see,' she said slowly, 'it began when Kyle's brother, Kevin, gave up his dream of going to medical school because he decided to get married. Had to, really. His girlfriend was pregnant.'

Amber stared at Rose in bewilderment. 'Kyle has a brother? I didn't know. But still, I don't see——'

'You will,' said Rose sadly. 'The baby miscarried, only by that time Kevin was working at the mill because he didn't want to work with his father. The marriage didn't work out, but he never did renew his dreams of becoming a doctor. He said it was too late. Then two years ago, when he was only thirty-three, there was an accident at the mill—and Kevin died.'

CHAPTER SIX

AMBER'S finger, which had been rhythmically circling her cup, stilled abruptly. 'He—died?' she said slowly. 'Oh, no. Poor Helvi. And poor Reijo. No wonder he has all his hopes and ambitions pinned on the son he has left.'

'Yes, that's just it. But his brother's death took Kyle quite differently. I think it brought home to him that life can be—unpredictable. And he saw that Kevin had never fulfilled a dream or done anything that really mattered to him. Instead he had tried to do the right thing in order to please other people, which in the end had all been a waste. He'd pleased nobody, not even himself—and he was dead.'

Amber nodded, and her red-gold hair fell across her face so that Rose couldn't see her eyes. 'Yes,' she said. 'Yes, I see. And of course Kyle was right, wasn't he? Kevin's life was a waste.' Rose said nothing, and presently Amber added, 'But I still don't understand why Kyle decided to throw away his career. Unless— was driving a coach a *dream*?'

Rose smiled wryly. 'Yes,' she said, 'ever since he was a kid. Other kids want to be pilots or spacemen. But not Kyle. *He* wanted to drive a coach. But, of course, it was a dream he gave up as soon as he started college. At that time he dismissed it as boyish non-sense. Then, when Kevin was killed, he became very cool and distant for a while. Nobody could get near him.'

'Can they ever?'

Rose laughed. 'He can be a bastard, can't he?' she agreed. 'But really he'd always been very approachable up till then. A bastard—but still approachable.' She grinned. 'Anyway, when he came out of his detached phase he announced that he was chucking the university in favour of a coach.'

'Forever?'

Rose shrugged. 'One never knows with Kyle. Maybe he's just working something out and will return to the academic life eventually. But—well, quite honestly, I think he's thoroughly enjoying himself doing exactly what he wants.'

'So do I,' said Amber, remembering Kyle's emphatic statement that he wouldn't drive a coach if he didn't like it.

'Mmm. But it's tough on Helvi—and on Reijo particularly, I think. He's beside himself.'

'Yes. And Kyle's very fond of both of them, isn't he? Although they can't expect him to live his life for them.'

'No. And Helvi doesn't. But Reijo likes things his own way—*and* he expects to get them.'

'Like father, like son,' murmured Amber into her teacup. She took a long gulp, and as soon as she put her cup down again the waitress arrived with their lunch.

It was getting late, and they were hungry, so egg salad on rye occupied their attention for the next few minutes. When they had finished, and Rose had licked the last alfalfa sprout from her lips, she said that now they really must get on with some shopping.

Amber chuckled, already knowing Rose well enough to realise that if shopping was on the agenda there was no point in trying to continue a serious conversation.

Hours later, tired and, in Rose's case, laden, they returned to the pick-up with their purchases. Amber had made only one—a 'Born to Shop' T-shirt for her new friend. It was received with good-natured laughter, and both young women were in high good humour by the time they arrived back at Flatrock.

'You've been shopping,' said Helvi accusingly as her eagle eye fell on Rose's booty.

'Just a little,' admitted Rose, with an engaging grin.

'A little, she says. You must have been at it all day.'

'Oh, no,' said Amber quickly. 'We went to Kakabeka this morning. It was breathtaking.'

'Kakabeka? Hmm. And how about Trowbridge Falls, Boulevard Lake, Chippewa——'

'Next time, Mrs Maki, I promise.' Rose's eyes were bright with sincerity.

'*Next* time. I know your next time, Rosie. You couldn't stay away from the shopping malls if you tried.'

Rose, deciding retreat was the better part of argument with Mrs Maki, gave her another deceptively charming grin and drove off.

'That girl.' Helvi shook her head. 'Well, that settles it. I'm busy tomorrow, but in a couple of days my boy can just come off his high horse and take you around himself.'

Helvi did not give up easily.

For the next week everything at the mine ran smoothly. Kyle was polite and distant to Amber, while Reijo seemed more resigned to his son's idiosyncrasies and gave up trying to make him change his job. The shop was always full of people, but Amber still felt a vague emptiness which she couldn't quite put her finger on. With will-power and sheer stubbornness she managed to convince herself that this feeling had nothing to do with Kyle.

One day near the end of the week, she left the cabin immediately after supper, saying she was going for a walk. She had no special destination in mind, but her feet moved in the direction of the amethyst cave which she hadn't visited since the day she had become stuck in the mud.

She was standing with her back to the entrance, her fingers exploring the crystal clusters on the wall, when she felt a light touch on her shoulder. She gasped, jumped and spun around.

'Sorry. I didn't mean to startle you,' said Kyle, not sounding very sorry at all.

'It's all right,' said Amber warily. 'What are you doing here?'

'Gracious as ever,' murmured Kyle, with the familiar edge to his voice. 'Mother sent me.'

'Oh, does she want me?'

'No. She might have appreciated an offer to help with the dishes, though. But I suppose you don't do dishes, do you?'

Amber gaped at him, confused as well as contrite. 'Oh, dear. No, I don't usually. But—well, I helped *you* do them that first day, didn't I?'

'Because I'm an incompetent male? And Mother can manage on her own?'

She wondered if he was right—if she had fallen automatically into the subservient feminine role she so disapproved of just because Kyle was a compelling and very sexy man.

'I don't know,' she said truthfully. 'I didn't mean to leave everything to your mother. I'm afraid I just never thought . . . I'm sorry.'

Kyle stared at her intently, and suddenly her genuine distress and bewilderment hit him like a blow between the eyes. And something he couldn't remember having felt before began to tug painfully at his heart.

'It's all right,' he said, cupping her cheek in his hand. 'I shouldn't have been so judgemental. I'm afraid I never thought, either. Of course, you don't ever have to do dishes at home, do you?'

'No. Neither does Mother. But *your* mother——'

'It's all right,' he said again. 'I helped her with them. I always have. I had no choice when I was a kid, and now it's become a habit.' He smiled, and it was a friendly smile, not censorious at all. 'You always run away right after supper, kitten, so of course you wouldn't know.'

'Yes, I didn't want to intrude, so I *have* been leaving, but . . . what must your poor mother think?'

'She likes you, believe it or not. Maintains you're a good worker and a decorative asset to the shop. So there you have it, little rich girl.' He smiled, a strange, almost bitter smile, but it made Amber's stomach turn over.

And his fingers were stroking her cheek.

'Don't call me that,' she whispered.

Their eyes met, and Amber saw his expression change slowly. The piercing eyes became deep sapphire pools as he bent towards her. Then both his hands were on her face and his lips were firm against her mouth. Without even wanting to respond, Amber found herself raising her arms.

But already it was over. He kissed her hard, purposefully—and very briefly. Afterwards his hands dropped to his sides and he turned away from her, passing his fingers distractedly through his hair.

Then he began to swear. Quietly, feelingly and for an unusually long time.

Amber, whose stomach had now returned to its proper place, listened with interest for a while, but when he started at the beginning again she broke in.

'Impressive, Mr Maki. Quite impressive. But you've said that already, you know.'

Kyle's tirade ceased instantly and there was silence. Then gradually his eyes, which had seemed almost dark with anger, cleared and became their normal striking blue. He smiled, a cool Maki smile. And Amber laughed.

'You're right,' he said, shaking his head. 'If one can't swear inventively, one shouldn't swear at all.'

'Especially in front of a lady. That's me, in case you hadn't noticed.'

His eyes gleamed appreciatively. 'Can't say I had, to speak of. Amber—I'm sorry. Listen, if I promise to keep my hands off you, will you come sightseeing with me tomorrow?'

Amber eyed him doubtfully. 'I don't know. I don't actually mind about your hands, but your mother——'

'Mother insists. On your coming, I mean.' His lips quirked. 'She doesn't know about the hands.'

'I should hope not.'

So Kyle had come to find her because Helvi had got her own way, as she usually did. That explained it, then. Amber felt a stab of disappointment.

'All right,' she said flatly.

'Good girl. And Amber...'

'Yes?' She could see that he was serious now.

'*I* mind about the hands. And I'm very sorry I kissed you—again. It *won't* happen any more. OK? Can we be friends?'

'Friends? I suppose so.' Resentment pricked some-where at the back of her mind. 'But I'm sorry that you're sorry you kissed me. It's not very flattering, you know.'

Kyle gave a short, mirthless laugh. 'Don't fish, kitten. You know you kiss very well.'

'So do you.'

'Thank you.' He bowed sarcastically and hit his head on the rockface.

Amber covered her mouth with her hand and Kyle, seeing her, lifted his hand threateningly. There was a glint in his eyes now that she didn't trust at all, and she stepped quickly to the back of the cave.

His hand stalled in mid-air and then came to rest above the entrance. 'Scared of me?' he taunted, running his eyes provocatively over her body as she stood with her hands flattened behind her against the wall.

'No, of course not.'

'You should be. You can't get away from me, you know.' He raised his other arm and stretched it across the opening so that any hope of escape was blocked off.

'So what?' said Amber scornfully. 'You wouldn't try to stop me in any case.'

'Try me.'

'Well, you wouldn't. You promised not to touch me. Remember?'

'Hmm. You have a point.' Kyle's eyebrows drew together and his fingers tapped thoughtfully against the rock. Then, without warning, his face cleared and his lean features lit up with a devilish glee. 'I re-member I said I'd keep my hands off you. But I never said anything about the rest of me, did I? Want to try and get past?'

'No.' Amber glared at him, not quite sure how far he might be willing to go.

Kyle grinned. 'You could be trapped there forever. Like the girl in the amethyst legend.'

'What legend?' scoffed Amber.

'Haven't you heard it? You see, the god Dionysus threatened to set his tigers on a young girl—whose name was undoubtedly Amber—and when she called to the goddess Artemis for protection, Artemis sealed her in crystal rock. Not very helpful, in my opinion. Anyway, Dionysus, overcome with remorse, poured an offering of wine over the girl and the crystal was stained purple, and became amethyst. So watch it, kitten. Or I may set my tigers on you, and you'll end up in a rock where you belong.' He smiled reflectively. 'Amber and amethyst. It wouldn't be inappropriate.'

'You do talk a lot of nonsense,' said Amber, with a resigned shake of her head. 'Tigers, indeed. You don't even own a cat.' The connection with Dionysus wasn't all that far-fetched, though, she reflected. Her very first impression of Kyle had been that he looked like a god.

He wasn't looking very godlike now, though. In fact, he was pulling a face at her and insisting that, if he didn't actually have any tigers at home, he had a very *large* ginger cat.

'Have you really?' asked Amber, interested. 'In Toronto?'

'Yes. Christina looks after her for me while I'm away.'

Oh, yes. Christina. She was always forgetting about Christina. 'Ginger cats don't count,' she said firmly. 'Now, will you please let me get by?'

The brittle note in her voice told Kyle that the game was over. He stood up, moved to the side, and left the way clear for Amber to walk past, which she did with her nose in the air. Come to think of it, he mused, Amber's pretty nose spent a lot of time in the air.

'See you tomorrow,' he said softly as her arm brushed against his. 'Nine o'clock on the dot.'

'I do wish you'd stop talking like an alarm clock!' snapped Amber. She also wished she could stop snapping at him, but as usual he had managed to put her out of sorts.

Since it seemed much easier to be ready on time than to listen to Kyle's strictures on punctuality, Amber was attired in her favourite jeans and blue T-shirt well before nine o'clock. And she took considerable satisfaction in informing him when he arrived that he was exactly one minute late.

He accepted this justifiable rebuke with surprising mildness, and in no time at all they were in his car and, as usual, speeding along the highway.

'First stop Ouimet Canyon,' announced Kyle a short time later, as they pulled into a parking spot beneath some trees.

'I don't see any canyon,' objected Amber, as he grabbed her hand and began towing her along a de-serted, bush-lined path.

But she soon saw what he was talking about, as they came out on to a rocky promontory high above the thick, flat, basalt sheets of the towering canyon walls.

'Amber!' shouted Kyle.

'Amber, Amber, Amber,' came back an echo from across the aeons-old chasm at their feet.

'Oh!' cried Amber, delighted. 'Oh, Kyle...'

'Kyle, Kyle, Kyle.' The echo was laughing at her, and Amber looked up at Kyle and laughed too.

Quite naturally he put his arm around her waist, and she leaned her head against him. Neither of them even remembered his promise about his hands.

As they walked back along the path, still linked together, Amber thought that she might never find a better moment to tell Kyle that she knew about his brother. Hoping she wouldn't break the spell, she took a long breath and said quietly, 'Kyle, Rose told me about Kevin. And that he was why you decided to drive a coach.'

'Did she? Yes, that was a bad time for all of us. Especially for my parents, of course.' He spoke quietly, too, not sounding as if he minded that she knew.

'And for his wife?' suggested Amber.

'Linda?' He looked surprised. 'Oh, by then that silly child was long gone. Didn't Rose tell you?'

'She said the marriage wasn't a success, I think, but somehow I had an idea they'd kept trying to make it work.'

'Not Linda. The moment something went wrong she went running home to Mama.'

'Oh. It must have been—awful. The break-up, and then Kevin's death . . .'

'It was. Still is.' He broke stride for a moment, and his fingers tightened on her waist.

'Yes. I . . . I can understand now why you made what—on the surface—seemed such a—well, such a startling decision.'

'Can you? But it wasn't all Kevin, you know. There were other considerations—problems.'

'Christina?'

'Good lord, no.' He stopped abruptly. 'Christina is the one person in my life who causes me no problems whatsoever.' He started walking again, and added reminiscently, 'But there *was* a woman before her. It was all over by the time Kevin died, but I suppose I hadn't quite recovered from the tragic grand finale.' He smiled derisively. 'I'm over-dramatising. It was low comedy, really. I'd had a few drinks that night, but if I remember rightly Leila hit me on the head with a telephone and I hit her back with a shoe.'

'You didn't?'

'Well, I'm not sure, quite honestly. But if I didn't, I certainly should have.'

'*Kyle!* You're talking more nonsense, aren't you?' accused Amber.

'Not exactly.' His eyes were shadowed now, fixed on some painful memory of the past. 'Kevin did die just after the blow-up with Leila. But in fact I'd been thinking for some months that I needed to get away, to have time to myself just to stand and stare—and think. You get a lot of staring time waiting at coach-stops.' He grimaced. 'As you must have noticed. At the university I was always besieged by people and problems, always battling the bureaucracy, involved in the politics...I needed time to make some decisions.'

'And have you made them?'

'I think so. At the moment I'm driving a coach.' His voice was clipped, permitting no discussion.

'So your decision was the right one.'

'Yes. For myself, if not for others.'

The chipped glass look was in his eyes again, prompting Amber to say quietly, 'You mean your father, don't you? So will you go back to your other life—some day?'

'You think I ought to, don't you?'

His voice had an icy note now, and Amber, not wanting to spoil the moment, said quickly, 'No, of course not. Let's talk about something else.'

She looked up, smiling, and saw that he was regarding her with a curiously cynical look in his bright blue eyes—and that his lips were twisted unpleasantly.

'You're going to be a toad again, aren't you?' she sighed, removing his hand from her waist.

Kyle choked, and the unpleasant look vanished without trace.

'Very probably,' he agreed solemnly. 'Am I a convincing sort of toad?'

'Very,' replied Amber succinctly.

Kyle laughed, and the thorny subject of his job was dropped by mutual consent.

They spent the rest of the day seeing all the places Helvi wanted them to see, and afterwards Amber remembered it as an almost perfect day. Whether it was because of Kyle's company or the scenery or the cheerful, shining sun, she was never sure, but whatever the cause she was happy, and she knew that Kyle was, too.

They talked about books and her family and his ginger cat and how much she liked Thunder Bay, and late in the afternoon they arrived at a secluded spot on the banks of Current River.

To Amber's surprise, Kyle produced a large paper bag from the back of the car. 'What's that?' she asked suspiciously.

'Food. Are you hungry?'

'Oh. Yes, I suppose I am, now you mention it.' She cast a dubious eye over the bag which showed ominous signs of splitting. 'You know, that bag ought to be a hamper,' she informed him, 'and you should be wearing white trousers and a boater.'

'Good grief.' Kyle shuddered. 'In that case, you should be wearing a wide-brimmed hat and a long white dress with frills.'

Amber giggled. 'What a grisly thought.'

'Oh, I don't know,' he mused. 'I think you'd look quite fetching in a hat and frills.'

'I wouldn't. I'd look like a drowned rat after I tripped over the hem of my dress and landed in the river because I couldn't see beyond the hat brim,' responded Amber prosaically.

Kyle laughed. 'I disagree. The prospect of you draped in clinging wet white, my dear, is even more alluring than the frills.'

'Lecher.' Amber aimed a playful slap at his face, but Kyle caught her smartly by the wrist.

'Don't do it,' he advised. 'I invariably hit back.'

'Yes, I know. With a shoe.' She smiled mischievously, and Kyle said she was a minx and let her go.

After a while he produced crusty French bread and a bottle of red wine, along with pâté and an enormous water-melon.

'Mmm,' approved Amber. 'Wonderful. How did you know I love water-melon?'

'I'm clairvoyant, after all, perhaps?' He leaned back on a long flat rock and linked his hands behind his head. ' "A jug of wine, a loaf of bread——" '

'But no water-melon,' objected Amber. 'You'll have to do better than that, Kyle.' The truth was, she didn't care what words came out of his mouth, but she had to say something to keep her mind off the long, virile body stretched beside her, to stop herself from reaching out to put her hand on his chest, just where the V of his dark blue cotton shirt opened to hint temptingly at what lay beneath ...

Desperately she shifted her eyes from the tanned skin covered with fine blond hair until they came to rest on his forehead. She saw that a small patch was beginning to turn purple where he had hit it on the wall outside the cave.

'Purple suits you,' she laughed, touching it gently with her fingers.

'Ouch. Hands off,' he ordered. And then both of them were silent, not wanting to admit that the prospect of 'hands on' was infinitely more attractive.

Darkness was already descending when at last they packed up the picnic and returned to Flatrock. Reijo and Helvi were just getting ready for bed. Helvi waved at them as they climbed out of the car and Amber saw that her expression was almost relieved. She wondered if the relief was due to their survival of Kyle's driving, or to the fact that he had brought her safely home without, apparently, having found it necessary to seduce her. She decided it was probably the driving, because surely Helvi knew enough about her son to trust his morals?

Unfortunately, thought Amber with regret, her trust was not one bit misplaced.

'Goodnight, Amber,' said Kyle softly, as they stood outside her trailer.

'Goodnight, Kyle. Thank you for a wonderful day.'

'I enjoyed it, too.' He hesitated, then placed both hands on the wall behind her head, so that she was trapped against the door. After a while he said quietly, 'I'm leaving on Saturday, Amber. Will you have dinner with me again before I go?'

'I—yes. Thank you. Of course I will.'

'Good.' He twisted a lock of her hair round his fingers, gave it a gentle tug, smiled and let her go. 'See you tomorrow.'

And that was all. Amber watched him walk away from her, saw the light go on in his trailer, and, with a sick, empty feeling in her chest, stumbled across the trailer to her bed.

Damn! She picked up her pillow, raised it above her head, then thumped it down again. What was the matter with her? She'd had a fantastic day, Kyle had been charming—most of the time—and she had no reason whatsoever to feel depressed.

All right, so she had wanted him to kiss her and he hadn't. But she had known all along that the day would end this way. Kyle had made it very clear that he had no intention of becoming seriously involved, so he was probably right not to start what he couldn't finish. Anyway, she didn't want to become involved, either. She wasn't in love with him, and she had always felt that sex and love should go together.

She knew where the truth lay, though. She was so much attracted to Kyle that her need for him had become an almost physical ache. Hormones, she thought disgustedly, picking up the pillow again. Then she realised that she had had this conversation with herself before. Obviously it hadn't done much good.

And Kyle would be leaving on Saturday.

Saturday. Flatrock wouldn't be the same without him. It would be so—flat. Yes, flat, but a lot more peaceful, she told herself bracingly. You'll be much better off without him, Amber Jones.

She was still telling herself that, with less and less conviction, when she finally fell asleep at four a.m.

*   *   *

Because Friday would be Kyle's last night at home, he suggested that Amber should have dinner with him on Thursday. When the time came for them to set out Helvi waved them off down the track with a beam that almost split her face, and Reijo remarked to his wife that for once that boy was showing a bit of sense.

'What did he mean by that?' asked Amber, who had overheard him.

Kyle sighed. 'Don't laugh, but I'm afraid visions of grandchildren dance through his head any time I'm seen within half a mile of anything female and presumably reproductive.'

Amber didn't feel like laughing. 'Thanks,' she said tartly. 'I suppose I do fit those qualifications.'

'Yes, and a few more besides.' Glancing sideways at her, he saw the stiff expression on her face and added softly, 'Don't sulk, kitten, I was paying you a compliment.'

'Some compliment,' scoffed Amber. But the stiff expression vanished and she smiled and asked curiously, 'Don't you like children, Kyle?'

He swung the car expertly round a bend in the road. 'Certainly I do, on those rare occasions when they're not screaming, whining or wetting. I must say I prefer them smiling and dry.'

'Mmm. I could say the same about some adults I know,' responded Amber.

'No doubt.' Amusement flickered at the corner of his mouth. 'And you? Do you like children?'

Amber laughed, a little self-consciously. 'I think I do, but quite honestly I've never had much to do with them.'

'No baby-sitting?'

She shook her head. 'No, I've never needed to baby-sit.'

'Poor, deprived Amber,' murmured Kyle.

'If you start that again I shall kick you,' said Amber viciously.

'And if you kick me we'll end up in the ditch. And then I shall kick you back—in precisely the right place.'

'Toad,' muttered Amber. It really was hopeless trying to get the better of Kyle.

This time he took her to a different restaurant, one which had dancing as well as a magnificent view of the lake.

'It's perfect,' she smiled, as they were shown to a secluded corner by a huge bay window and Kyle helped her into her chair.

'I'm glad you approve. The décor almost matches your dress.'

It did, too. The walls were a soft leaf-green and Amber's dress was of clinging emerald silk. Like the red one she had worn earlier, it was cut very low at the back. There wasn't much to the front, either. The skirt sheathed her hips like a fitted doeskin glove, and with her hair swept back behind her ears in a very plain gold clasp she hoped that she looked both sophisticated and bewitching. Kyle seemed utterly determined not to cross any physical barrier between them, but it would be their last time alone together and she had no illusions about her own desires. She wanted him to kiss her again, and she would do everything she could to make it happen. When she saw his eyes roam appreciatively over her figure, slim, and curved in all the right places, she knew that she had made a good start.

He, too, looked incredibly seductive, and a little overwhelming, in a dark grey suit and a blue shirt that matched his eyes.

At Amber's suggestion, Kyle ordered for both of them. They had perfectly cooked rare steaks, salad, and tiny fried potatoes that melted in her mouth. She was glad that when the wine came Kyle tasted, nodded and accepted it nonchalantly, without making a great production of it as so many of her father's friends did.

'That was wonderful,' she said, as they finished with pecan pie for dessert. 'Just exactly right. And you haven't been a toad even once.'

'Watch it, kitten.' Kyle eyed her severely. 'The night is young yet—and if you're not careful I'll do what my mother suggested and make you walk all round the fort.'

Amber stared at him. 'What on earth are you talking about?'

He grinned. 'Apparently during our sightseeing tour the other day we missed Mother's favourite spot. Thunder Bay's contribution to Ye Olde Canadian Fort industry. You know, no city worthy of the name can be without one.'

'Oh, I see,' laughed Amber. 'Yes, Winnipeg has one, too. Old Fort Garry.'

'Naturally. And Thunder Bay has old Fort William, in case you didn't know. Very educational. A walk might do you good.'

'*Not* after a large meal, thank you. Anyway, it's too late to threaten me with forts now, you idiot. It's already getting dark.'

'So I'm an idiot, am I?' he said softly. 'Just for that I'll make you get up and dance.'

For some time the small band had been playing soothing dinner music, but now it increased its tempo as a few couples got up to dance.

'Come on.' Kyle pushed back his chair and imperiously held out his hand. Amber placed hers in it, and he led her on to the floor.

Kyle danced as she had known he would, with a cool, sinuous grace that sent shivers up her spine. And into her limbs and down to the pit of her stomach. He was not touching her, just moving and twisting his body in a slow, sensuous rhythm that made her blood begin to sizzle. She followed him, bending her body in time with his, and as they circled the floor the music became louder, more suggestive, and it matched the sensations that Kyle's nearness was arousing in every tingling nerve-end.

His hypnotic blue eyes locked with hers and held them as, slowly and inevitably, they came together.

Kyle's arms went around her waist, drawing her against him, and as they danced, barely moving now, Amber could feel the tough male length of him moulding her to him through the silky green softness of her dress. Then the music slowed to a dark, erotic beat that made her feel as if her body were in flames. But they were curling, voluptuous flames that made her twist longingly in his arms, press her soft body against the hardness of his chest, wanting to be closer, to be one with this man who could stir emotions and sensations that she had never even imagined.

She wrapped her arms around his neck, clinging frantically, as she felt his hands slip lower, stroking the smooth green silk, then cupping her thighs to pull her even closer. And then, as his mouth finally descended over hers, she could no longer hear the music. She could hear nothing, see nothing, was conscious of nothing but Kyle—and his lips and his tongue and the athletic hardness of his supple body...

The band finished the set with a crash, and there was silence.

Slowly Kyle lifted his head, his eyes still glazed with desire. 'We'd better get out of here before we make a worse exhibition of ourselves,' he growled, in a voice that was harsher than she had ever heard it.

Amber nodded. 'Yes. All right.' She was having trouble catching up with her breath.

Kyle seized her hand, almost dragged her back to their table to collect her bag and wrap, and in what seemed like only a split second they were outside, breathing unevenly in the warm, scented summer air.

Amber glanced up uncertainly at his face, wondering what she would see there. And she knew at once that she had been right to wonder, because the aquiline features were cold now, almost rigid, and the nostrils of his long straight nose were flared as if he were the villain in some old, forgotten melodrama.

'Why are you looking like that?' she asked cautiously, wanting to touch him and knowing that it might be unwise.

At that, with a quick, frustrated movement, he turned away from her and flung up the bonnet of the car.

'Because I let myself do it to you—after I swore that I wouldn't.' He slammed the bonnet down again and faced her, brushing his hand impatiently across his brow. When he lowered it, she saw that his forehead was smudged with thick black oil.

'You didn't do anything to me,' she assured him, as he swore under his breath and reached inside the car to find a rag.

'I did.' He spoke curtly, wiping the oil from his fingers with a grim concentration. 'Amber . . . I don't know what's going on in your mind, but I think we have to talk.'

'I agree,' she said quietly, wondering what he thought was going on in her mind and why his words had somehow given the impression that he didn't think it was likely to be much. She felt a small spark of indignation, and decided to hang on to it. She might need a dose of good old-fashioned temper to get her through the rest of this night.

A few minutes later they were once again parked by the river, not far from the place where they had sipped wine and eaten water-melon only a few days before. But now it was dark, and only the occasional white flash of the water reminded Amber of that happier time.

'It's private enough here,' said Kyle, with frost in his voice.

'So it is. Why the big chill, Kyle? What have I done now?'

His fingers tapped rhythmically on the dashboard, and he didn't look at her when he answered. 'Nothing, I hope. I don't want to hurt you, that's all. Amber... I have every reason to know that you're a very—passionate young woman, but—oh, hell!' His nostrils flared again and he stared distantly out of the window.

'But what?' asked Amber steadily.

'But...' He took a deep breath. 'Amber, you're not to fall in love with me, do you understand? Because there's no future in it.' He was facing her now, and one hand was gripping her shoulder as his eyes fastened on her face.

Amber gaped at him, and as the first shock wore off the anger she had been saving up spilled over. 'You arrogant bastard!' she said scornfully, not knowing why it was important to hurt him. 'Whatever gives you the idea that, just because you're a very attractive man, every woman you meet is going to fall in love with you?' She tossed her hair back and it stroked his hand on her shoulder so that he released her abruptly. 'If you want the truth,' she went on, 'I *did* think about having an affair with you—and then I thought better of it, because I *don't* love you. Two kisses—or was it three?—do not a lifetime commitment make, Kyle Maki. Enjoyable though they were.'

'Oh, yes,' said Kyle bitterly, his voice cutting like diamonds. 'Oh, yes, I know you enjoyed them.' He stared at her, his eyes now as cold and bright as his voice. 'But as long as they were just your idea of an amusing way of passing the time, there's nothing to worry about, is there?'

'Oh, Kyle.' Something in the way he spoke cut through the anger she had adopted as a shield, and she wished more than anything that this conversation had never begun. They seemed to communicate so much better in other ways...

'Kyle,' she went on doggedly, 'this is stupid. We have nothing to quarrel about. You kissed me, and I liked it. I'd like you to do it again. There's nothing wrong with that, and you're leaving the day after tomorrow. Why can't we be friends?'

'Friends?' Kyle shook his head. 'I hoped for that, too, at first. But tonight has brought home to me in spades that I want more than friendship from you, Amber.' He lifted his hand towards her, then let it drop back across the wheel.

'What more?' asked Amber doubtfully. 'You don't want love. You said so. Which,' she added, with a resurgence of her old spirit, 'is probably just as well, since I'm not ready for it, either.'

Kyle sighed. 'Use your imagination, kitten.' His voice was very dry.

'Oh,' said Amber, as the light dawned. 'Oh, I see. You want my—my...'

'I want your beautiful body, Amber darling,' Kyle finished bleakly. 'And as I've no intention of taking it, I would find it very hard to be "just friends".'

'I see,' murmured Amber, wondering why she had a sudden infuriating urge to cry. 'Well, just in case you hadn't noticed, Kyle *darling*, it wasn't offered to you. So you don't have a thing to worry about, do you?'

Kyle's mouth twisted. 'Wasn't it?' he asked softly. 'I thought it was.'

Amber glared at him. He was right, of course. If he had suggested stopping at a hotel on the way home tonight, she would probably have said no to him. But in the end she wouldn't have been able to resist. And he knew it. Smug, impossible, gorgeous bastard. Already she could feel those sensual stirrings again, clawing away at her somewhere deep inside.

She swallowed. 'Look,' she said, 'you have a point. I do find you devastatingly attractive. And apparently you feel the same way about me. Both of us agree it isn't love. At least, not yet. But is there any reason why we can't keep in touch, see each other sometimes and just—see what comes of it?'

'Yes,' said Kyle harshly. 'There's every reason. I'm twelve years older than you are, Amber. Half my students were your age, and I'm not about to be accused of cradle-snatching. These affairs just never work.' He moved away from her and leaned his head back on the window. 'My judgement may have been temporarily clouded because—because you're a maddeningly seductive little witch, but I am *not* so irresponsible as to let it go any further. You're only a kid, for heaven's sake. And I couldn't live with myself if I hurt you.' He passed a hand wearily across his eyes.

Amber, watching the thin lines tighten around his mouth, knew that he meant every word of it.

'These things do work sometimes. Quite often, in fact,' she said dully. 'My father is thirteen years older than my mother and they're quite satisfied with each other. But obviously if you're going to persist in thinking of me as an oversexed delinquent, there's not much more to be said.'

'Amber! I didn't say——'

'No, of course you didn't. It's what you were thinking, all the same. Please——'

'No,' he interrupted harshly. 'No, Amber, it's *not* what I was thinking.'

'Please take me home, Kyle.' There was no point in arguing with him any more.

'In a minute. First I have to make you understand.'

'What's there to understand?' she asked drearily.

'That I don't for a moment think you're an over-sexed delinquent. I think you're an intelligent, desirable woman. But a very *young* woman, Amber. It's not just that I've seen too many disastrous liaisons at college, although heaven knows there were enough of those sordid little affairs. But you see—it happened in my family as well.'

'What do you mean?' Not that it mattered. His mind was already made up.

'Kevin, my brother, got involved with a girl younger than himself, and you know how that turned out. She was only eighteen and it ruined Kevin's life. They were desperately unhappy, and it distressed my parents more than I can say. In the end that marriage killed

Kevin, because he wouldn't have been working at the mill if he hadn't met Linda.'

Kyle's eyes in the faint light from the moon were opaque and looked very far away, remembering past tragedy, and at first Amber didn't know what to say.

Then she murmured in a choked voice, 'Yes, I see. I understand why you feel as you do, Kyle. But—history doesn't always repeat itself. I'm twenty-two, not eighteen, and I—I only want us to be friends.'

She saw the white flash of his teeth in the darkness as the river flaked white behind him. 'Friends?' he repeated, for the second time that night. Briefly his hand brushed her cheek, and was withdrawn. 'Yes, I'll be your friend, Amber. I wish you happiness. But after I leave here I'm never going to see you again. It wouldn't be fair to you.'

'Or to you either, I suppose,' she said bitterly. 'The truth is you're afraid to take a chance.'

'Am I? Maybe.' His lips drew into a thin, hard line, and Amber knew that she had lost.

'It's getting late,' she said tonelessly. 'I think we'd better go home.'

He opened his mouth, started to say something, then turned abruptly away from her. With his face as grim and set as she had ever seen it, he turned the key and started up the engine with a roar.

They drove back to the mine in silence. A tense, half-angry silence alive with unspoken words, and it continued right up to the moment when he left her at her door. There he bade her an abrupt goodnight, making no attempt to touch her, and vanished so quickly that she had trouble believing that he had ever been with her at all.

Two days later, in the middle of a torrential summer downpour, Kyle hugged his parents, shook hands coolly with Amber, stepped into Erik's car—and was gone.

CHAPTER SEVEN

It was only after Kyle had left that the truth hit Amber.

During the twenty-four hours before his departure, she had been so conscious of the fact that he was near, and might appear to set all her nerves screaming at any moment, that she had been incapable of coherent thought. When she did finally see him again, casually eating supper with his parents, her face turned a fiery red the moment she stepped through the door.

Helvi noticed it and looked pensive. Reijo noticed it and looked unmistakably hopeful. Kyle appeared not to notice at all and politely pulled out a chair. And that was how it continued. He was distant, controlled and excruciatingly polite. He smiled at her, but the smile never touched his eyes, and as soon as the meal was over he said he had to pack.

Amber only saw him once again, briefly, when Erik arrived to drive him into town and Helvi called her from the shop to say goodbye.

And that was when it hit her.

The rain had stopped as quickly as it had begun, and she saw the sun flash brightly on Kyle's fair hair as the car disappeared round the corner. And then she knew.

She didn't want to be Kyle's friend any more than he wanted to be hers. She wanted to be his love. But he had gone from her life forever, and because of that it would never be the same again.

She hadn't wanted to fall in love with him. She had thought she was telling the truth when she'd told him she *didn't* love him, and in the end it had made no difference. Cupid was not remotely concerned with her wishes. He had put Kyle in her path, and the inevitable had happened. Oh, yes, it *had* been inevitable, she saw that now. She just hadn't been willing to accept it. It wasn't only that Kyle was impossibly sexy and attractive. It was the way he teased her, made her laugh, liked the same things she did: books, cats, rare steaks, the Northern Ontario scenery, Erik and Rosie—and amethyst.

But Kyle was gone, and she was back in the shop now, without quite knowing how she had got there. Absently she picked up a shimmering mauve ring and placed it on her finger.

She would never wear Kyle's ring, she thought with a wrenching sadness, as she twisted the stone to catch the light. Oh, he liked her well enough, wanted her even, but certainly not for his wife. In fact, he was so convinced that she was just another of his eagerly nubile students that he wasn't even willing to be her friend—because she might lead him into temptation. So it didn't matter that Cupid had shattered her well-laid plans, did it? Since Kyle refused to interfere with them anyway, she could continue on her chosen path. She would get her degree next year, find an interesting job with a mining company or the government, where perhaps she could use her English skills as well as her interest in gemology, and...

No. That was where the whole scheme came unglued, because after the job her plans had included marriage, at a suitably mature age, to a man who loved her and had needs and ambitions similar to her own.

Well, she had found that man, hadn't she? But from his point of view her age wasn't suitable at all. He didn't love her, and his needs and ambitions were in no way similar to hers. So he had gone away. By the time she came to the marriage phase of her scenario, Kyle would probably have married the calm, undemanding Christina—who always looked after his cat.

All right, thought Amber, catching a tear on the edge of her tongue and tasting salt. All right. So wedding bells are out. I'll just have to settle for a good degree and a job.

Blindly she tore at the amethyst ring and ripped it off her finger. It grazed the skin, leaving a red raw weal.

'Damn,' she muttered, plunging it into a tub of water. Then she realised that the water was full of mud and swore again, to the gleeful amusement of a group of high-school students who came in at that moment and decided that educational tours were looking up.

Two more weeks passed, then three. The rain continued on and off, and one day slid into the next without much meaning, and soon it was the end of July.

Amber performed her job quietly and efficiently, read the books she had brought with her and helped Helvi with the dishes in the evening—but she found that every time she wiped a plate she was reminded of Kyle, who had said he always did dishes. Helvi, who continued to watch Amber reflectively when she thought she wasn't looking, said that Kyle had phoned to tell her that everything was going well in Toronto. Apparently he had found both his apartment and his cat in good condition.

'Yes,' said Amber. 'Of course. Christina.'

'I expect so. She's a good girl.' Helvi shook her head. 'But very independent.' She gave Amber a quick, probing glance and added, 'He asked after you.'

'Kyle did?' Amber's heart gave a wild and unnecessary leap.

'That's right. I told him you were doing fine—but that you had become very quiet since he left.' The bright, probing look became more pronounced than ever.

'Oh,' said Amber, flustered. 'Am I quiet?' She laughed self-consciously. 'That's not the complaint I usually hear about myself.'

'It's not a complaint, my dear.' Helvi dumped the last dish on to the draining-board and pulled out the plug with a squelch. 'Yes, you *are* quieter than you used to be. You ought to get out more, you know.'

Oh, dear. Was the heaviness in her heart as obvious as that? 'I am going out tomorrow,' she said quickly. 'Rosie has asked me for dinner. Is that all right?'

'Certainly it's all right. You need to be around young people more. The change will do you good.'

Yes, thought Amber. Of course. That's what I need. A change. I need to be somewhere where I won't be reminded of Kyle whenever I look around me—and see places where he was, and objects which he touched...

But when Rose picked her up and drove her to the small neat house beside the highway, the first thing she said after getting out of the truck was, 'You look pale, Amber. And you're much too subdued. What's the matter? Is it Kyle?'

'Wh-what?' stammered Amber, who had never quite got used to Rose's bluntness. 'What do you mean? There's nothing the matter with me. And, anyway, why should it be Kyle?'

'Because it invariably is. I grew up with that boy, remember, and I know the signs of a chronic attack of Kyle when I come across one. I suppose I'm just lucky that I never succumbed myself.' She shoved her truck-keys into the pocket of her trousers and began striding towards the house. 'Is it terminal?'

'Is *what* terminal?' sputtered Amber, running to keep up with her. 'You talk almost as much nonsense as Kyle does, Rosie.'

'The attack, of course. Are you going to recover?'

'Oh, Rose,' exclaimed Amber, stopping in her tracks. 'You're a tonic. Yes, of course I'm going to recover.'

For the first time since Kyle had left her, she actually wanted to laugh.

By the end of the relaxed, cheerful evening with Rose and Erik she was beginning to believe that life might be bearable after all. Some time in the future surely she would be happy again, and if she waited long enough perhaps she would even find the sort of contentment that Rose and Erik shared. It wouldn't be the same as loving Kyle, of course, but at least she was ready to . . . ready to what? Hope? Yes, that was it. It was just a matter of getting on with her life, making the best of things and taking advantage of whatever chances of happiness came her way.

Which was why, when Harry Jones phoned the following evening and asked to speak to his daughter, she was almost excited as she ran across from her trailer to take the call. Usually conversations with her father ended in disagreement, but this time she was optimistic. She knew Harry well enough to know that he would not have phoned unless he had plans for her—and for once she was inclined to fall in line.

After all, one never knew. Maybe whatever her father had in mind would be just what she needed to take her mind off Kyle. If that were possible...

It turned out that Harry was staying in Thunder Bay.

'You are?' squeaked Amber. 'But I thought you left for Paris two weeks ago.'

'Changed my mind,' said Harry. 'Bit of business came up. Thought we'd spend a few days over this way instead. Chance to see how you're getting along, Amber—do some fishing...' He cleared his throat.

'Yes?' said Amber, knowing there was more to come. 'And...?'

'Jack and Pierre Lavalle are down here with me.' Harry's voice was deceptively non-committal.

'Oh?' replied Amber, deliberately not reacting. 'What about Mother?'

'Still in Winnipeg. She's involved with some charity function or other, and couldn't get away.'

Yes, thought Amber. Mother's no fool. She knows all about sitting by rocky lakesides watching Dad not catch any fish. Or sitting in hotel rooms waiting for him to get back in a bad temper from not catching any fish. 'I see,' she said quietly. 'When can I see you, then?'

'Thought you might come in for dinner tomorrow night.'

'Just the two of us?'

'No—no. The Lavalles will be with us, too.' Again that deceptive lack of inflection—and now Amber knew exactly what this phone call was all about.

'All right,' she said. 'That will be great. I'm afraid you'll have to pick me up, though.'

'Mmm, yes. Of course. I've rented a car. Young Pierre drove down in his Porsche.' He paused as if waiting for her response. When it didn't come, he added, 'Must pay my respects to the Makis. Haven't seen them for years.'

No, she thought, and you wouldn't be seeing them now either if you hadn't managed to persuade the Lavalles to come with you on what's supposed to be a fishing trip. Well, it was fishing in one sense, all right, only she, Amber, was the bait.

For over four years now her father had lost no opportunity of throwing her and Pierre Lavalle together because Pierre was his 'right young man'. Harry's intentions were obvious and his methods unsubtle, but his dreams of a match between the Lavalle and Jones families were at least partly based on genuine concern for his daughter—as well as a desire to enhance his own prestige. Jack Lavalle owned a highly successful land development company in Winnipeg, and if Amber married his son her money allied to the Lavalle fortune would ensure her a wealthy and worry-free future. That was what Harry believed at least, and Alida Jones shared his opinion.

Amber herself was not so sure. Pierre was handsome and civilised, and he always did the right thing socially, but she had noticed that he never seemed to have any real interest in anyone except himself. All the same, she didn't dislike him. She was as indifferent to him as she suspected he was to her. And she had no intention of marrying him.

Still, she thought quickly, as Harry waited for her reply, even an evening with the Lavalles and her father would be better than sitting alone in her trailer dreaming useless dreams of Kyle.

'See you tomorrow, then,' she said brightly.

Harry hung up the phone with a grunt.

The following day, fishless as usual, but only slightly short-tempered, he arrived to pick Amber up almost as soon as she had closed the doors of the shop. While her father had a few obligatory words with the Makis, she changed hastily into the first thing she laid her hands on: a skin-hugging jumpsuit in shimmering pale mauve silk.

'You sure that mauve item is all right for dinner?' asked Harry Jones as they drove away. 'Looks very— hmm—casual to me.'

'It's fine, Dad,' said Amber firmly. Not that she cared one way or the other. Dinner with the Lavalles was not her idea of a super-significant occasion.

However, when they arrived at the hotel, and for the first time she saw something which looked very like hopeful lechery in Pierre's dark, handsome eyes, it did occur to her that her father might have been right after all. Maybe the jumpsuit did fit a little too well.

Dinner conversation was mainly a long drawn-out post-mortem on the day's fishing—or lack of it—and Amber was having a hard time keeping her eyes open by the time Pierre leaned over and murmured into her ear, 'Shall we leave them to the fish tales, Amber? I'll take you for a drink.'

Harry caught the end of his words and looked satisfied. Jack smiled slightly and went on talking about fish.

What the hell? thought Amber. Anything's better than the fish tales—and Pierre *is* tall, dark and handsome, and very smooth, and he's looking at me with gratifying appreciation. What have I got to lose?

It didn't altogether surprise her to find out that Pierre had some fairly definite ideas about what she might have to lose, to him, and preferably tonight.

'Not a chance,' she said lightly, sipping her third pink gin in the dimly lit bar of the hotel.

'Why not? After all, it's on the cards that we're going to marry one of these days. We've known each other for years, and I'm not——'

'Oh, I know. You're not unattractive,' admitted Amber, who after wine and three drinks was beginning to feel pleasantly hazy. 'But this is the first I've heard about us getting married.' She put her head on one side and gave him a boozily coquettish smile. 'I don't think you've even proposed to me, have you, Pierre darling?'

'No, well, plenty of time for that——'

'And I don't see why you want to marry me, anyway. You're not in love with me, are you?'

'I like you; I think you're very pretty; our parents approve; we'll have a very nice fortune between us. In short, I think we'll suit.'

Amber giggled. 'Is that supposed to be a proposal, Pierre, my love?'

'Of course not.' Pierre had the grace to look sheepish. 'No, Amber, when I propose to you I'll do it properly. Candle-light, wine and roses, soft music——'

'And will you go down on one knee?' asked Amber interestedly. Her body slid sideways in the chair. She really was beginning to feel a little odd.

Pierre stared at her in alarm. 'I shouldn't think so,' he said hastily. 'Amber, are you drunk?'

'You know, I really think I must be,' said Amber, grinning broadly. She wasn't *that* drunk, but, judging from the disgusted expression on Pierre's face, it was a good way of warding him off.

'Right,' he said resignedly. 'That's that, then. Is your father going to take you home?'

'I think he hopes you are.' She hiccuped.

Pierre sighed. 'Of course. Delighted. Come along, then.'

A few minutes later, after saying goodbye to her father and Jack and expressing hopes to meet them again before they returned to Winnipeg, Amber was snugly ensconced in Pierre's Porsche. They purred along the highway in what in Pierre's case was disappointed silence, and in Amber's sleepy forgetfulness. Pierre was all right, she thought tolerantly. She didn't love him, but then he didn't love her, either. At least he was honest. And Kyle was a long, long way away...

She closed her eyes.

'Shall I see you tomorrow?' asked Pierre, as he held open the door of the car half an hour later.

'I don't know,' yawned Amber. 'Maybe.' She fumbled for the key in her white beaded evening bag.

'You wouldn't remember anyway, would you?' said Pierre with a note of acidity in his voice.

'Probably not,' she agreed drowsily. 'Thanks for bringing me home.'

'My pleasure. Goodnight, Amber.' With a slight tightening of his lips Pierre turned away.

Fifteen minutes later Amber was asleep, and for once she didn't dream of Kyle. In fact, she didn't dream of anything at all.

The next morning she thought she must be dreaming, though. She woke up with a screaming headache, and as she grovelled in the cupboard above the sink for an aspirin she heard the faint squeal of the door opening behind her. Had she forgotten to lock it, then? She must have. Not surprising. But— who would be coming in at this hour? She wasn't due in the shop for another forty-five minutes.

Pushing her tangled hair out of her eyes, she turned slowly. Then one hand went to her mouth and the other, futilely, to the neck of the blue cotton nightdress which seemed to be slipping off her shoulders.

'What...?' she gasped. '*You*—I don't understand...'

'No,' said Kyle, his blue eyes flicking over her. 'As a matter of fact, I'm not sure I understand myself. You look terrible, Amber. Not at all the sort of sight a man wants to wake up to in the morning.'

CHAPTER EIGHT

'Thanks,' Amber managed to sputter, as joy, disbelief and confusion mingled with a familiar sense of outrage. She made another unsuccessful grab for the neckline of her nightdress, but the short, gathered sleeves only slid further down her arms.

'Don't mention it.'

Amber's grey-green eyes narrowed. 'Besides, there's no danger of your waking up to me in the morning, is there?'

'I don't know. That's what I came back to find out.'

Pain stabbed rhythmically at the back of her head and she put up her hand to relieve it. The nightdress dropped even further. 'What are you talking about?' she asked tiredly. 'And why did you walk in without knocking?' It wasn't what she wanted to say, but rational thought and speech had been washed away the moment he had come through the door. And her head wouldn't stop pounding.

'I walked in because the door was open. And I thought I was talking about us.' Kyle's voice was as cool and seductive as it had always been, and Amber gave a little gasp and instinctively held out her arms.

In one stride he was in front of her, and his hands were on her shoulders—reaching down. For a moment she thought he was going to push the nightdress on to the floor, but instead he caught the sleeves in his tapered masculine fingers and pulled them gently back to where they belonged.

'There,' he said softly. 'It's not an improvement, but I don't think I could carry on any kind of a conversation with you standing there naked, impersonating Venus in the early morning.'

'I thought you said I looked terrible.'

'Yes, but just now I wasn't looking at your face.'

'Which *does* look terrible?' The headache had receded for the present, and her voice held a trace of indignation.

Kyle cupped her chin in the fingers of one hand and turned her head to the light. 'Ghastly,' he confirmed. 'What in the world have you been doing to get in a mess like that? Misbehaving yourself, from the looks of you.'

'I wasn't. I had dinner with my father,' said Amber righteously, hoping he wouldn't remove his fingers from her chin. She liked him here, standing close to her. His thigh was touching her hip, and, in spite of her head and the general weakness in her limbs, it was intoxicating. *He* was intoxicating.

'Your father? Does he always have this effect on you?'

'No, of course not, it wasn't that.' Suddenly she felt giddy, and although he was still holding her she found that she had to sit. Unwillingly she moved away from him and sank down on to the bed.

'It wasn't my father. It was afterwards—with Pierre.'

Was it her imagination, or did the thin lips harden slightly? There was certainly a glitter in his eyes.

'Pierre?' he repeated evenly. 'And who is Pierre?'

'Pierre Lavalle.'

'Of course. That explains everything.' The sarcasm in his voice was exaggerated and unmistakable, as she was sure it was meant to be.

Amber glared up at him, her hands twisting in her lap. But glaring hurt her eyes, so she closed them. The pain was back with a vengeance.

'Pierre's the son of a friend and business associate of my father's, if you must know,' she told him, not bothering to hide her exasperation. 'Dad hopes we'll get married one day.'

'I see. And will you?' There was no sarcasm in his voice now, only a sort of wary control, and when Amber looked at him closely she saw that the tanned face had gone a strange, mottled white. But brown couldn't turn white, could it . . .?

She shook her head, and wished she hadn't as a hundred needles stabbed her behind the eyes. 'No,' she gasped painfully, 'of course not. But he's in town with father, and I had dinner with them, and afterwards Pierre bought me a few drinks.'

'I thought so.' Kyle rested his fist on the cupboard over the sink and stared down at her. 'And you, like an idiot, drank them.'

'Yes,' said Amber, in a small, choked voice. 'But I very much wish I hadn't.'

In a flash Kyle was beside her on the narrow bed, his white-shirted arm around her shoulders. For a while he just held her, not moving. Then he turned his cheek and laid it on her hair. 'Poor little kitten,' he murmured softly, as he caressed her shoulder lightly with his thumb.

When Amber, after a second of startled hesitation, turned to look up at him, she saw that he was smiling. But it wasn't a malicious smile, only a tender, very gentle amusement. And as they sat there, he with his arm about her and she with her head on his shoulder, both of them became aware of a sensation of warmth and peace and rightness—and soon, of something else which was very much more than warm.

It was a need, a hot, passionate need, and Amber was no longer aware that she had a headache.

Abruptly Kyle dropped his arm and drew away.

'Right,' he said authoritatively. 'It's back into bed again for you, young lady.'

'No,' exclaimed Amber, as Kyle's hands caught her by the bare ankles and swung her legs up on the bed. 'No, Kyle, you can't——'

'*I'm* not going to, charming thought though it is.' He sighed regretfully. 'No, Amber, my dear, *you're* going back to bed—by yourself—and I'm going to run the shop for Mother. She's helping my father at the mine and she's enjoying herself, so I know she won't want to leave.'

'Oh, but you can't. I mean, that's not fair. It's *my* job——'

'Yes, and if you'd refrain from acquiring hangovers on sexy junkets with your boyfriend you'd be able to do it a lot better,' he said grimly. 'So shut up and sleep it off, and I'll be back this evening to take you out for a strictly sober dinner.'

'Bread and water, I suppose,' murmured Amber meekly, eyeing the taut lines of his face with resignation. 'And Pierre is *not* my boyfriend.'

'Bread and water is more than you deserve,' he said severely. Then, seeing her big eyes fixed with beguiling innocence on his face, he gave up the heavy uncle act and smiled. 'I'm glad he's not your boyfriend.'

Amber smiled back contentedly. Her head already felt better as it settled back into the pillows. 'What *are* you doing here, Kyle?' she asked idly, not caring as long as he stayed. 'You're supposed to be off somewhere driving a coach at the moment, aren't you?'

'I've got a long weekend. So I came back.'

'Why?' She held her breath.

His hand smoothed the hair back from her forehead. 'Because I wanted to see you. I missed you, Amber. I couldn't believe how much.'

'What about Christina?'

'I told you before. Christina is just a friend now.'

'Really?'

'Really. But, you see, every time I went out with someone else I kept wishing she was you.' He grinned ruefully. 'You've ruined a great many promising opportunities for me, kitten. In the end I decided maybe you were right when you said that age didn't have to matter. Perhaps I *was* just afraid to take a chance, and that's not an attitude I particularly admire. Also, when I stopped to think about it, I realised that half the people I know are several years older or younger than their partners, and the fact that it didn't work for Kevin didn't mean it couldn't work for me.' He paused and then added sheepishly, 'In fact, my mother is five years older than Dad.'

'Is she really?' I never thought about it.'

'That's just it. People don't, do they? But I was— blinded, I suppose, because I'd taught so many pretty young women and a lot of them did get into involvements without really knowing what they were doing. Sometimes I had to pick up the pieces. You have to understand, Amber, that at first *you* were just another know-it-all kid to me.'

'I can't blame you. I *was* pretty horrible, wasn't I?' said Amber complacently.

'Mmm. Quite revolting. But you're not really just a pretty, brainless young woman, are you? There's a lot of sense under that cloud of coppery hair.' He touched it, almost reverently. 'And you were right, too, when you said we should give it time, get to know each other . . .'

Amber smiled up at him dreamily. 'I think I know you already, Kyle.' She put out her hand and ran it along his thigh.

He picked it up and placed it firmly back under the covers. 'Don't do that, kitten, or the shop won't open and your headache will get considerably worse.'

'No, it won't. It'll get *much* better.' She stretched out her hand again, and Kyle jumped hastily to his feet.

'Behave yourself,' he ordered, 'or I'll make you get up and run the shop yourself.'

'You couldn't be so heartless. Not after telling me I can spend the whole day lolling about in bed—while you do all the work.'

'You're asking for it, aren't you?' He took a step towards her, and his eyes held a threatening gleam.

'No,' said Amber quickly. 'I'm not. I'll be good. I always am.' She tucked both hands under the covers and gave him a look of such doe-eyed innocence that Kyle stopped short, laughed, and shook his head.

'How do you do it?' he wondered. 'Nobody looking at you now would believe for one moment that your Pierre got you drunk last night. Well—apart from a few bags under your eyes, and that green look around your ears——'

'My ears are *not* green. And Pierre is not "my" Pierre.'

'Truly, Amber?' He was serious now.

'Very truly, Kyle.'

He nodded, satisfied. 'Good. Now, do as you're told and sleep. I'll see you about six.' He leaned over her, kissed her lightly on the tip of her nose, and left.

Amber stared at the closed door through which he had disappeared, and smiled happily. Life was going to be wonderful, after all.

She watched raindrops escaping down her window as the sun came out from behind a cottony cloud.

And then she fell asleep.

When she woke up it was already five o'clock, but her headache had completely gone and her limbs felt as if they belonged to her once more. She smiled happily. Kyle would be coming to fetch her in an hour.

Amber threw back the bedclothes and jumped out of bed with more energy and enthusiasm than she had shown in over a month. Kyle was back. He had missed her. She had been right to believe in the future, even though until today she had given up hope that it would ever again contain the man she loved.

She glanced at the clock he had given her. Too late now to get over to the cabin for a shower. It was probably occupied anyway, so she would just have to wash very thoroughly.

That done, she began to rummage in the tiny cupboard. What to wear? Her eye fell on the pale mauve jumpsuit, and she remembered the effect it had had on super-civilised Pierre. Yes. The jumpsuit would do very nicely, especially as she had reason to know that behind his cool exterior Kyle had interestingly primitive urges. She had always thought he bore a certain resemblance to a wolf...

She had just finished dressing, and was rummaging through her make-up, when she heard a quick, sharp rap on the door.

Her eyes widened. It was only twenty to six. Kyle must be early. Well, he'd just have to wait while she tidied her hair and put her make-up on. Her eyes very bright, and smiling a welcome, she hurried to let him in.

But it was not Kyle who stood waiting on the damp ground outside. It was Pierre. And he, too, was smiling. As Amber studied the handsome figure, tall and imposing in an impeccable dark suit, and carrying a bunch of roses, she realised with a stab of consternation that his smile was expectant and proprietorial. Oh, lord. *Had* she told Pierre she would go out with him tonight? No, surely not. It was true that she had not been quite herself when she had left him, but she distinctly recalled him saying, rather unkindly, that she wouldn't remember it even if they did make a date.

'Good evening, Amber. Aren't you going to ask me in?'

He was still smiling, and it was the sort of smile that showed he had no doubts about his welcome. He expected her to be pleased to see him. Which she wasn't. Kyle would be arriving shortly and she still had to finish her face.

'Well, Amber?' Impatience was now mingled with expectation.

'I—there's very little room in here,' she said feebly.

'That's all right. I'll make myself small in a corner while you get ready.'

'Yes, but—ready for what?' Her hand reached behind her for support and found none.

'To come out with me, of course. Amber, are you going to let me through that door, or do I have to push you out of the way?'

'Oh. Yes. Well—all right.' She stepped back hesi-
tantly, and Pierre took her by the shoulders, moved
her in front of the mirror and sat down carefully on
the recently made-up bed which Amber still had not
bothered to lift against the wall. She glanced quickly
to her right to make sure that the door behind them
was open.

Pierre held out the roses. 'For you, Amber.'

'Oh. Thank you.' Amber took them uncertainly,
and began to search for a vase. There wasn't one, but
she found an empty jam-jar. 'Pierre...'

'At your service.'

'Pierre, I can't go out with you tonight. It's very
kind of you, and the roses are lovely, but——'

'Of course you can. You're not working, are you?'
He made the word 'working' sound like a childish
game.

'No, I'm not. But I *do* have other plans.'

Pierre's eyebrows rose in disparaging disbelief. 'In
this dump? My dear Amber, you must be joking.'

'I'm not joking and it's not a dump and I'm going
out with Kyle.' She turned angrily away from him and
started to brush her hair.

'Who or what is Kyle?' he asked, amused contempt
evident in every syllable.

'He's—his parents own the mine,' she replied
shortly—

'Oh, I see. One of the local yokels. Come on,
Amber, you know your father wouldn't like it. I'm
sure you just meant to be kind to the fellow, but
really——'

'Kyle is *not* a local yokel,' said Amber, putting down
the brush and turning to face him. 'He's a man I—
like—very much. And he's taking me out tonight—
which you're not. Listen, Pierre...'

But Pierre was not listening. He was looking. And his eyes, as they ran insultingly over her body, had a very unpleasant glint in them which she didn't trust at all.

He stood up slowly.

'Pierre...' she warned, as he took a step towards her. 'Pierre, no!'

But it was too late. Her body was pressed up against the sink now, and Pierre's hands were on her waist, bending her backwards.

'Come on, Amber,' he said softly. 'Drunk last night, out with the locals tonight. Don't try and kid me I'm assaulting your dubious virtue. All I'm asking for is a kiss.'

His mouth was very close to hers now, and she could smell alcohol on his breath. Cognac, if she wasn't mistaken. And she had thought he was civilised, the perfect social foil!

'Amber?' he repeated, his warm breath slithering across her cheek. 'Just a kiss, lovely-Amber-in-the-sexy-jumpsuit. Then perhaps I'll leave you to your yokel.'

His hands were tightening on her waist and her back was beginning to hurt where it was pushed against the sink. And Kyle would be coming soon. Oh, she didn't want him to walk in on this sordid little scene. If only Pierre would leave her alone.

'Would you go away if I let you kiss me?' she asked doubtfully, hating the feel of his lips against her cheek. They were nice lips really, but the wrong lips. 'Would you, Pierre? Please?'

'All right. I will if you kiss me back, sexy Amber. Just for old times' sake.'

'But there haven't been any old times,' she protested.

'Then kiss me as a pledge of future, less chaste, delights.'

'There isn't going to be any future. Pierre, *please* let me go.' She put her hands against his chest and tried to push him away, but he only moved closer so that she was pinned between his body and the sink.

Oh, what did it matter? she thought desperately. It wouldn't be the first kiss she hadn't enjoyed. And if she gave in to him now, he had promised he'd go away. The door was open, it couldn't possibly do any harm . . .

'All right,' she said resignedly. 'Let's get on with it, then.'

She closed her eyes and nothing happened.

'I said you had to kiss *me*,' his thick voice murmured in her ear. 'Put your arms around me, Amber.'

Amber swallowed, inhaled deeply, and did what he wanted. Then she touched her lips very lightly against his.

Instantly his arms moved around her back, crushing her against his chest, and his mouth on hers became hard and seeking, demanding what she had never intended to give.

She made a sound that could have been a cry of passion, but was only a plea for help.

Then, incredibly, as she tried to tear her lips away and fought frantically for breath to resist, a voice from the doorway said icily, in a tone that cut like a whip, 'Well, well, well. What a very touching reunion. Roses, I see. I do admire your taste, Amber. But surely you could have picked slightly more—glamorous— surroundings for this rather *squalid* little interlude? And I really would suggest you close the door.'

Slowly Pierre's arms dropped from her waist and he released her. Amber rubbed the back of her hand across her lips and stared in frozen horror at Kyle while her unwelcome suitor turned round to inspect the source of the interruption.

'Who are you?' he asked rudely.

'As this is my family's property, I suppose I might ask the same question of you,' drawled Kyle unpleasantly. 'However, I don't think it's necessary, as you'll be leaving very soon. I presume that's your Porsche in the car park?'

'What's that got to do with you?'

'Nothing much. I was just making sure you have transportation. Because you're going to need it. Get out.'

Amber saw that the muscles in Kyle's lean face were pulled taut with an anger that was barely controlled. His lips were drawn back in a sneer that made him look more like a wolf than ever, and his eyes ... his eyes were as cold as glass on a winter's day. Blue glass. Glass like very thin ice. And Amber shivered.

Pierre's well-shaped mouth fell open slightly, making his profile look fishlike. Amber wondered why she had once thought him attractive. Compared to Kyle, standing tall, magnificent—and furious—in the doorway, he was thoroughly insignificant. Even so, he showed no inclination to back down in the face of a superior physique.

'Why should I get out?' he asked belligerently. 'This may be your land, I suppose, but Amber is my girl.'

'Pierre!' wailed mber.

'Like hell she is,' rasped Kyle.

'Oh, do stop it, both of you!' cried Amber, trying again. 'You're behaving just like two dogs snarling over a bone.'

'No,' said Kyle, giving her a glacial stare. 'Like two dogs snarling over a bitch, perhaps, but I would never call you a bone.'

She could see that his anger was still held tightly in check, but now her own emotions, which had been on a roller-coaster over the past few weeks, erupted into blinding rage. So he thought she was a bitch, did he? Well, he'd discover she could be just that.

'Shut up!' she shouted. 'And get out. Both of you. All right, so this is your property, Kyle Maki, but it's my home as long as I'm working here, and you can keep your charming opinions of me to yourself. As for you——' She rounded on Pierre, but before she could start on him he interrupted.

'Steady on now,' he said placatingly. 'No need to get upset. I'll leave in just a moment, Amber. That is, if you're sure it's safe for me to leave you with this, this . . .' He tried to stare down his nose at Kyle, but it proved difficult, because the other man had at least two inches' advantage.

'*This,*' said Amber bitingly, 'is your local yokel, Pierre.'

'Ah.' Pierre pulled at the cuff of his jacket and lifted his eyebrows in disdain. 'I see. The one you are going to dine with.'

'No,' said Amber, her voice still choked with anger. 'No, Pierre. I most certainly am not.' Then she added in a quieter tone, 'I'm not dining with anyone tonight. So will you please, please just *go*?'

Pierre looked at her, his eyes momentarily bewildered, then he passed a hand over his forehead, nodded, and replied with surprising dignity, 'All right. Sorry about all this, Amber.' He made a vague, ineffectual gesture with his arm and stepped towards the door which Kyle still blocked. Pierre paused, and

Amber could see why. Kyle looked impressive and overwhelming and almost menacing, towering there in a dark suit with his hands clenched on the door-frame. To complete the picture of power about to explode, heavy grey clouds were gathering behind his head. Her heart began to thump so loudly that she wondered if they could hear it.

Oh, lord, surely Kyle wouldn't refuse to move?

He didn't. Instead he stared hard at Pierre for what seemed a very long moment. Then his body shifted with catlike fluidity, his mouth twisted in a sneer of bitter contempt, and Pierre, with a last, confused glance back at Amber, slipped quickly around him and made his way to his car. As he passed, Amber saw Kyle curl his fingers forcibly against his thighs.

She stood mesmerised for a moment, her eyes following Pierre's rapidly departing figure. Then she said dully, not looking at Kyle, 'You'd better go too now, hadn't you? There isn't much point in your staying.' The anger she had felt a few minutes ago had been replaced by an enormous weariness.

'I think not.' Kyle stepped into the trailer and kicked the door shut behind him. It closed with a sharp, convincing click.

'Kyle,' said Amber, in a voice that was devoid of emotion, 'Kyle, really there's no point . . .'

As he paid no attention, but continued to advance towards her, she added despairingly, 'Oh, no, not you, too. I've been through this once already this evening.'

His hands were already grasping her upper arms, but now he was suddenly still. 'You've been through *what* already this evening, Amber?'

Looking up into his coldly furious face, Amber found herself shivering again. Not from fear of him, but of the bleakness she saw in his eyes—and which

she knew must be mirrored in her own. The bleakness
that was born of loss and a deep sense of emptiness.
But it was no good. She couldn't change what had
happened.

'Oh, I haven't been through what *you're* suggesting,' she answered bitterly. 'I was talking about
kisses taken out of juvenile revenge. Because that's
what Pierre was doing. He was hurt because I turned
him down.'

'What I saw and heard did not look in the least
like "turning him down". Don't lie to me, Amber.'

'So now I'm a liar as well as a bitch, am I? Aren't
you going to go all out and call me a slut? Before you
kiss me.'

'What makes you think I'm going to kiss you? And
no, I wasn't going to call you anything quite so old-
fashioned. Although I can think of more modern
words that might apply.'

'Then if all you're going to do is call me names, I
really see no reason for this discussion, or for you to
be here, or—oh, for heaven's sake, Kyle, why won't
you go *away*?' Her body sagged hopelessly beneath
his fingers, which were still holding her by the arms,
and as she moved a lock of her hair fell forward on
to his hands.

He stiffened, drew in his breath, and then said grat-
ingly, 'Because I promised you dinner. And I keep my
promises, Amber.'

'Meaning I don't?'

She looked up at him tiredly, surprising a look she
couldn't understand. There was anger, certainly, confusion, and was it—pain? Then it passed and there
was only the anger.

'I don't know what you keep, Amber. But I imagine that men who own Porsches and are approved

by Daddy are not lightly to be thrown away—in favour of the local yokel.'

In an instant all Amber's weariness vanished, and was replaced by overwhelming rage. How *dared* this arrogant man accuse her of lying to him—or worse— and of selling herself to the highest bidder? Because that's what it amounted to if he thought she would marry Pierre because he could give her money and social standing.

'You bastard,' she said very quietly. 'You utterly unspeakable bastard.'

She raised her hand and slapped him, hard, across the face.

He didn't attempt to stop her. Instead he stood frozen, and as still as a marble statue. Then, as a red wound flamed across his cheek, he caught her wrist and pulled her against his chest while his other arm clamped around her waist.

His mouth closed over hers.

At first his lips were abrasive and angry, seeking revenge, just as she had accused. Amber, the adrenalin of rage still coursing through her body, tried to pull away to fight him off. But his arms only tightened. Both of them were around her waist now, and his hands were sliding over the smooth mauve silk of her thighs and bottom, pressing her relentlessly against him. And then, as she felt the hard male strength of him bending her along his sinuous length, desire, resented and unwanted, snaked through her body, and she stopped struggling and stood passive in his arms.

Immediately the feel of his lips changed, they became warmer, sweeter, quite irresistible, and he murmured her name in her ear. Amber's arms coiled around his neck to hold him tight, and her fingers touched his hair, grasped it, then moved slowly, sensuously across his back.

'Amber.' Kyle's voice was a hoarse groan, and before she knew how it had happened she was lying on the insubstantial bed and Kyle was lying beside her, half on top of her. And his jacket and tie were trailing on the floor.

She felt his hands at her neck, on the zip of her jumpsuit, and in a moment, as her fingers caressed his back, her lacy bra was down beside his jacket. His hands were on her breasts, then his lips, as his fingers feathered lightly over her stomach, arousing a heat and a need she had not known it was possible to bear.

'Kyle!' she cried out. 'Kyle. I love you.'

His body, so warm and desirable, went suddenly rigid and he lifted his head from her breast. Slowly he rolled away from her, then stared down in silence as if he couldn't believe what he saw.

After a long, frozen moment he sat up.

'Oh, hell,' he groaned, burying his face in his hands. 'Amber, I'm sorry. You're so beautiful—and I was so angry. Believe me, please, I didn't know what I was doing.'

'Kyle?' Amber stared at his back, mystified, her body still trembling with need and emptiness. 'Kyle, what is it?'

He turned to look at her now, his eyes very bright and hard. 'I'm sorry,' he said again. 'That was inexcusable.'

'No.' Amber shook her head violently on the pillow. 'No, it wasn't inexcusable. It was—would have been— wonderful.'

'Yes,' said Kyle bleakly. 'I expect it would. But I'm not in the habit of despoiling virgins. It's a principle of mine. Especially not when they're going to marry suitable young men with prospects.' His lips twisted cruelly.

'Oh, don't be ridiculous!' snapped Amber, the exhilaration of Kyle's lovemaking rapidly slipping away as she clumsily fastened her jumpsuit. 'I'm not going to marry Pierre. And you've got all the prospects you want to have. And it's not my fault I'm a virgin.'

'Really?' Kyle raised his eyebrows. 'Well, I've no idea what I'm supposed to make of *that* remark, my dear.' He sounded tired now. 'And as for your not marrying Pierre—what the hell was he doing here then, with roses, and why were you curled around him like Virginia creeper?'

'Kyle,' said Amber, the events of the day suddenly becoming too much for her, 'I'm not going to answer that. You can think what you like. And right now you can go away. Pluto will do nicely. I believe that's the furthest planet, but if you like I'll settle for Neptune.'

Kyle stared at her, his expression a mixture of disbelief, exasperation and—still that something else which she couldn't read. 'All right.' He shrugged. 'If that's what you want.'

It wasn't what she wanted, but it was all she could take at the moment. 'Yes,' she said. 'Yes, please go.'

Without another word Kyle picked up his jacket and tie, slung them over his shoulder, and, looking rumpled but achingly desirable, he closed the door behind him with a snap.

She got up automatically to lock it, then sat down on the bed and, as Kyle had done before her, she buried her face in her hands.

She was still sitting there half an hour later when there was a loud knock on the window.

CHAPTER NINE

'WHO is it?' she called, not caring.

'It's Kyle. Open up.'

'No. Go away.'

'You haven't eaten.'

'I don't want to eat.'

'Well, I do. Come on, Amber, I've come to take you out. You can't sit in there all night and sulk. I'm sorry if I—upset you.'

'I'm not sulking and you didn't upset me. Now go away.'

'Amber, do you want me to break the door down?'

'More caveman stuff, Kyle?'

A few choice words she hadn't heard before came zinging through the window. 'Amber, I'm warning you——'

'And I'm warning you. If you don't go away, I'll—I'll call your mother.'

He made a sound that came somewhere between a curse and a snort of derision. 'You'll tell my mother on me, will you? I haven't heard that one since Erik and I used to fight over the doughnuts we stole from Charmaine Oikenen's lunch-box.'

Amber decided that she wasn't getting into the matter of Charmaine Oikenen's lunch. It could remain a mystery of Kyle's nefarious past. 'I don't care,' she insisted. 'I'm *not* going out, and I *don't* want anything to eat.'

She didn't, either. Her stomach felt like coiled elastic bands and just at the moment she was in a

state of such mental confusion that she couldn't face
a further confrontation with Kyle. She wanted time
by herself to think.

There was silence outside the door for a few moments and then Kyle's voice, taut with irritation,
snapped, 'Suit yourself, then, madam. Starve. It will
do you good!'

It'll do me as much good as your bread and water,
she thought sourly. Then she heard stones crunch beneath his feet as he walked away.

Hours later, Amber changed her mind and decided
that she did want to eat. Not much, but enough to
assuage the pangs in her stomach which she supposed
must be due to hunger. At first she had thought that
they were just part and parcel of the pangs she felt
in her heart.

She heated a tin of chicken noodle soup, which
settled inside her like lead. Perhaps food hadn't been
the answer, after all.

Thoughts still swirled in her head in a kind of
mindless confusion, and the only thing she was sure
of was that she didn't want to see Kyle. Not now.
Maybe not ever.

Oh, she could understand his initial anger on seeing
her with Pierre. He was bound to jump to the wrong
conclusion, and, as she had promised to spend the
evening with him only a few hours earlier, it was only
natural that he should feel betrayed. But calling her
a liar, and later implying that she was no more than
a shallow social climber—those things were
unforgivable.

Only she had forgiven him, hadn't she? There had
been those timeless moments when she would have
forgiven him anything, handed him everything in the
world she had to give. And she had told him so. She

had said, 'I love you.' And immediately he had withdrawn from her, thrown her virginity in her face and almost goaded her to marry Pierre.

Why? She didn't understand him. On the one hand he had said he'd come back because he'd missed her. Then, when she had said she loved him, he had rejected her and told her to marry someone else. It didn't make sense. Unless—unless he had only come back to satisfy a physical urge, then when it came to the crunch his conscience had somehow managed to get in the way. Yes, she supposed that made a kind of sense. She should be thankful that he'd had his attack of morality in time.

But she wasn't.

No, that was wrong. She *was* thankful. Very thankful. It would have hurt ten times more if she had had him for an hour or two and then lost him.

She dropped a clean soup-bowl into a sinkful of soapy water, and put the dirty one absently back in the cupboard. And as she stood there, staring into space, hurt and indignation rose in her until she wanted to hurl open the door, run across to Kyle's trailer and—and—she didn't know what she wanted to do to him, but whatever it was it would hurt. As she was hurting.

In the end, of course, all she did was peel off the mauve jumpsuit, pull on her nightdress and tumble unhappily into bed. And to top it all off, she fumed, as she glared up at the ceiling and the list of Kyle's perfidies grew larger in her mind, to top it all off, he had even accused her of sulking. Well, she had a right to sulk. And to cry and kick and scream. If any of them would do her any good.

But for some reason she couldn't cry. Perhaps it would be different in the morning.

It wasn't.

When Amber woke up, after a restless, uneasy night, it was raining. And she felt the same as she had the night before. Hurt, bereft, empty—and, above all, angry.

It was the anger which got her through the day.

The weather kept most of the tourists away, so business in the shop was very slow, which she regretted. It would have been easier if she could have been so busy that she wasn't given time to think. As it was, she had very little to do except brood over the scene with Kyle. And the more she brooded, the more her rage at him mounted.

Just before five o'clock, as she was running a brush listlessly over an amethyst-veined rock, Kyle walked into the shop. She knew it was him without even turning around. But she went on brushing the rock, splashing mud-stained water on the floor.

'Amber?'

She didn't look up.

'Amber.' His tone was imperative now, permitting no evasion.

'What?'

'Look at me.' She could feel his hand on her arm, and there was no hope of avoiding him. Reluctantly she put down the amethyst and looked up.

'What do you want?'

He was wearing a thin black sweatshirt and, irrelevantly, she found herself admiring the long line of his muscular neck.

'I'm leaving in half an hour. Erik's driving me into town. I came to talk to you.'

So he was leaving, she thought dully. Well, that was good. 'There's nothing to talk about,' she told him.

'Amber...' He shoved his hands into the pockets of his jeans and rested his hip on a table. 'Amber, I know you're angry. I don't blame you. My behaviour was inexcusable, but I've admitted that already.'

'I'm not angry,' lied Amber.

He smiled, a twisted smile that just reached the edge of his lips. 'All right, so you're not angry. But I want to apologise—again—for making you not angry. I saw red when I found that fellow kissing you. If you want the truth, Amber, I was jealous. But I should have believed you when you said it wasn't your idea. I know you're not a liar. That's one of the things I like about you, your honesty.'

'I'm delighted to know there's *something* about me you like.' She picked up the stone and started scrubbing again—viciously. Kyle reached across and removed it from her hands.

'I'm talking to you. Pay attention,' he said quietly.

'Yes, *sir*.' Amber raised her arm in a snappy salute and for a moment, as irritation flared in Kyle's eyes, she thought he might retaliate physically. She looked anxiously behind her for escape and found only a tub of dirty water. Then the irritation faded and Kyle went on evenly, 'Amber, I called you a liar——'

'And a bitch.'

'And a bitch. And I suggested you would marry that man for his money——'

'Yes, I noticed.'

'Shut up. And, to round off a perfect score, I almost seduced you. I know that's not much of a record—or a recommendation—but do you think we can start over again?'

Amber stared at him, at the tall, slim body all in black, at the golden hair, the hypnotic eyes and the lean brown aquiline face she had come to love. And she remembered how he had looked last night, the blue eyes filled with contempt and the thin lips curled up in a sneer. She remembered how he had accused her of lying, of selling her charms to Pierre. And all the brooding, the fulminating anger which had been building in her all day, spilled over as she saw her chance to hit back. To hurt him as he had hurt her.

'No,' she said, very clearly and coldly. 'No, we can't start over, Kyle. I've decided to take your advice. I think I'll put my money on the man with the Porsche and the prospects.'

For a moment, when she saw the look in his eyes, Amber was genuinely frightened. She put her hands protectively behind her back. But Kyle saw, and the fingers of his right hand, which had been slowly uncurling, relaxed again as his arm fell back to his side.

'Don't worry,' he said impassively. 'You deserve it, but I'm not going to do it. Goodbye, Amber.'

He stared at her for a long time, his eyes running slowly over her body as if taking in every detail of her hair, her serviceable shirt and trousers and even the shoes on her feet. Finally they came back to her face. 'Goodbye, Amber,' he repeated.

And the next moment he was gone.

Amber stood rooted to the spot, unable to make her legs move. She opened her mouth, tried to say something, but no words came. Then, as she heard a car pull up in the distance, her limbs came suddenly to life. With a frantic, uneven gait she stumbled across the room to the door which Kyle had slammed behind him, opened it and screamed, 'Kyle!'

And she saw him pause with one foot on the running-board, turn his head so that he met her eyes, and then, very deliberately, ease his tall body on to the seat beside Erik.

Then Erik started the motor and they were off. And the rain continued in an unrelenting sheet.

'What's up, old friend?' asked Erik, after they had driven several miles in an uncomfortably crackling silence. 'Do I detect signs that the man with the iron heart has finally succumbed to feminine charms?'

'Mmm?' Kyle, who had been staring stonily through the window, turned an abstracted look on his friend.

Erik repeated the question, and Kyle smiled bleakly. 'You could put it that way. But I never was made of iron. I've succumbed many times before, you must remember.'

'Only when it suited you. I gather this doesn't suit.'

'No,' said Kyle, slamming the flat of his hand against the dashboard and causing Erik to jump and cross the median line. 'No, it doesn't. I couldn't have made a worse fool of myself if I'd tried.'

'But you didn't try?'

'No. I tried not to.'

It was true. He had tried very hard not to fall in love with Amber. Even though he had come back to Flatrock because he couldn't get her out of his mind, he still hadn't been sure. Well, he was sure now. She had made it very clear that she was not the girl for him. Or he the man for her...

Oh, yes, she had cried 'I love you' in the heat of passion, but she hadn't meant it. It probably amused her to keep two men on a string, but when it came right down to choices she knew that her bread was buttered on the side which her father had selected for her for years.

Yet she had called after him—and he had ignored her...

He shrugged. It was better that way. They had no more to say to each other.

Erik stepped on the accelerator and in only a few minutes they were on the outskirts of Thunder Bay.

Amber pressed her nose against the living-room window as she had done ever since she was a child. Soft heaps of new-fallen snow covered the lawn where it sloped down to the frozen river. It looked very clean and cold and—empty somehow, this postcard scene over which for once not a breath of Winnipeg wind was stirring the bare, stark branches of the trees.

Across the large, high-ceilinged room a small fire flickered in the centre of a big amethyst fireplace and was reflected in the tinsel baubles decorating a silver tree. At the front of the house she knew the scene would be quite different. Ridges of dirty grey slush pressed down by passing cars, and at the sides of the road mounds of cold, oil-grimed sludge.

But she had lived in Winnipeg all her life and she was used to its freezing, grey-white winters. Besides, the chill and the greyness and the cold, streamlined room matched all too well the coldness around her heart. That was why, to her parents' acute irritation, she had refused to go with them to the Bahamas for Christmas this year. She had told them she wanted to spend the festive season quietly with the family cats and Mrs Martin, the housekeeper, who had promised to stay with Amber because her own daughter wouldn't be home. Harry and Alida Jones had grumbled and cajoled, but in the end Amber had got her own way.

Now, watching the snow, her mind went back to those hot summer days at the mine.

She had thought, as the season passed and the end of her time at Flatrock grew near, that she would get over the loss of Kyle, at least to the point where life would seem worth living. But she hadn't got over it. At first she had believed, against all hope, that he would come back, if only to see his parents. But they told her he rarely came more than two or three times a year. The rest of the time he kept in touch by phone.

Once when he called she happened to be in the cabin, and she heard Helvi ask him if he wanted to speak to Amber. But the answer must have been very brief and negative, because there was hardly a pause before Helvi handed the phone over to Reijo.

Almost before Kyle and Erik had disappeared down the track on that disastrous rainy day, Amber had known that she had just made the biggest mistake of her life. She had let hurt and anger consume her to such an extent that she had driven away all her own hopes of happiness. Her unthinking rage had made her tell Kyle that she intended to marry Pierre. And he had said that he admired her honesty! That hadn't been honest, it had been false, childish and unbearably foolish and fatal. Now it was too late to do anything about it. She had seen the look on Kyle's face when she'd told him she would put her money on the Porsche and the prospects.

He despised her.

Many times since that day she had reached out her hand to phone him, but she always withdrew it again. If she called and he rejected her, as she was almost sure he would, then even the tiny glimmer of hope which never quite died would be extinguished.

You're a coward, Amber Jones, she thought to herself now, as her eyes roamed from the glowing fireplace to the chilly scene outside. You've been home for over three months now, and the pain isn't getting any easier. If you don't at least give yourself—and Kyle—a chance, you may regret it for the rest of your life.

And if I do, said another voice, I may regret it even more.

She stared at the fire for a long time. Then she went upstairs to her room with the blue and gold walls and the pristine single white bed, and stared at the phone. She sat for almost an hour looking at it, perched uncomfortably on the edge of her bed, and when at last she lifted her head huge flakes of snow were falling outside the window.

Snow. Cold. Grey skies. Was that all there was for her?

No, she whispered to herself. No, Amber. You *have* to try.

It was difficult talking to Helvi, who thought she had just phoned to wish her ex-employers a merry Christmas. When she asked, awkwardly, if Kyle happened to be there, Helvi said no, he was coming on Christmas Eve, but would Amber like his number?

'Yes,' she murmured. 'I would very much like it. Please.'

A few minutes later she could hear the bell ringing in his flat in Toronto as she sat with the receiver pressed tight against her ear.

It rang six times before he picked it up, and when he did he sounded impatient.

'Yes? Who is it?'

When she didn't answer he snapped curtly, 'Who is this?'

'I—it's—Kyle, it's Amber.'

There was silence on the end of the line, and then his voice came back, very cool and detached. 'Amber. What a delightful surprise. Merry Christmas.'

'Yes. Merry Christmas. Kyle...'

'Yes, Amber? What can I do for you?'

No emotion, no reaction at all. It was as if she were some vague acquaintance phoning to solicit a donation for disadvantaged cats, or homeless rodents. As if she were anything other than the woman he had almost made love to making a desperate appeal to his heart.

'I—I just wanted—I wondered...'

'Yes?'

'Kyle, I——' She stopped. There was another voice on the line, and it wasn't Kyle's. A woman's voice, and it was very close to the phone. Amber couldn't hear all she said, but the gist of the woman's words seemed to be that Kyle should keep the conversation brief. That was followed by a quick, high-pitched giggle.

'Amber?' Kyle's low, masculine voice sounded firmer now, less disinterested. 'Amber, hang on a minute——'

But Amber didn't hang on. She hung up.

Eight minutes later to the second—just about the time it would have taken him to get her number from Helvi—the phone rang.

Amber knew it was him. She sat and listened to it ringing, loudly, all over the house. It rang twelve times in all, but Mrs Martin was out visiting a friend and there was no one else at home. Amber didn't answer. After the twelfth ring, it stopped.

She stood for a long time gazing through the window at the snow and the darkening sky.

He wouldn't call again. He had someone else, and she had been a fool even to hope for a moment that he had spent the past months celibate and alone. She had given him no reason to, and he owed her nothing. Obviously her call had interrupted some passionate new affair. Christina might be a back number, but a man like Kyle would have no trouble finding a replacement.

Oh, sure, he had called her back, she was almost certain, but he would have done that automatically out of a sense of obligation, in case the suddenly dead connection had been a mechanical or electronic mistake.

But it hadn't been a mistake. She had found the courage to call him at last. And courage had come too late.

In just three days it would be Christmas.

Exactly six months later, Amber was seated on a plane thinking that in just three hours she would be in Toronto with dear Aunt Minnie.

Kyle was in Toronto. Maybe . . . No, she mustn't let her mind wander in that direction, because in that direction lay trouble. Not just because every time she thought of him her heart seemed to break in two, but because now she had Pierre to consider.

'Thank you,' she said, smiling briefly at the stewardess who was offering her a drink. 'I'd love one.'

Yes, now she had Pierre. Seven months ago she would not have believed it possible. But somehow, after that abortive call to Kyle, nothing seemed to matter much any more. Because she had always finished what she started, and because in spite of everything it was still important, she had completed her degree. So now she was no longer a student, but a woman with good prospects for a job. Somewhere between Christmas and her final exams, Pierre had appeared on the scene again, full of apologies for his behaviour in the summer and explaining that, in spite of all appearances, he was shy. That was why he had had too many drinks that evening in Thunder Bay, he said. To give himself confidence with Amber. Unfortunately it had worked a little too well.

Amber had accepted the apologies because she had nothing to lose, and eventually, to an accompaniment of candle-light, roses and wine, Pierre had asked her to marry him. She had refused. Then her father had found out, and there had been endless unpleasant scenes. In the end Pierre had asked her again, this time on a riverboat with an orchestra—and she'd accepted.

She still felt that she had nothing to lose, and her unhappiness was so great that she would have done anything just to achieve family peace and quiet. Peace and quiet were all she had left now, and she valued them. Besides, Pierre didn't pretend to love her any more than she loved him. He, too, was ready to please his father. They would make no demands on each other, but perhaps they could achieve a kind of companionship. And she would have her job. It would be all right ...

But she must never for a moment allow herself to think of Kyle. Especially she mustn't dream of seeing him again just because she happened to be in Toronto.

'Amber!' Aunt Minnie's cry of welcome was reminiscent of the day almost a year ago when she had come to collect her niece from the Buffalo coach. But this time there was no tall, arrogant coach-driver to carry Amber's cases for her, and after her initial beaming greeting Aunt Minnie began to look worried.

'Amber? You seem so much older—a little tired, dear.'

Amber smiled faintly. 'That's what you said last year, Aunt Minnie. I'm all right. And I *am* older.'

'Yes, but it's not that—has something happened to you, dear?'

Oh, yes, something had happened to her all right, and apparently it showed. But it wasn't anything she could talk about. Not even to Aunt Minnie.

An hour later she was sitting with her aunt on the back porch of her snug suburban home sipping a long, cool drink. It was blazing hot, as Toronto summers so often were, but Amber was as used to the heat as she was to snow and wind, and because the warm months lasted such a short time she enjoyed them. As much as she was capable of enjoying anything these days.

'So you're getting married.' Aunt Minnie's gentle eyes studied her over the top of her glass.

'Yes. Father's very happy about it.'

'I know. He even phoned to tell me before you did the day the engagement was announced.' Her eyes dropped down to follow the progress of an ant on a blade of grass. 'Are *you* happy, Amber?'

Oh, dear. There never had been much point in trying to hide things from Aunt Minnie. But still she had to try. 'Yes, of course I am,' she smiled.

'Your young man—you love him?'

'Aunt Minnie, I . . .' Amber hesitated, not knowing how to answer. 'What do you mean, do I love him? I mean, I'm going to marry him, aren't I?'

'Yes, I suppose you are, dear.' The ant fell off its blade and disappeared under the porch. 'But that doesn't necessarily...' She stopped, and gave Amber a look that was almost embarrassed. 'Dear, I know I've no right to intrude, but you *don't* seem very happy. Not like a newly engaged young woman ought to look at all. And that's another thing. Why did you want to spend two weeks here with me and Uncle Marty when you could have spent the time in Winnipeg with your young man? Or if your parents were worried about that, you could have gone with them to Europe.'

Amber shook her head, her mind suddenly flooded with memories of Kyle. 'Pierre and I have the rest of our lives to be together,' she said quietly. 'We won't miss each other for just a couple of weeks. And— Aunt Minnie, I'd rather be here with you than in Europe. I've always been so happy here.'

Amber didn't hear the break in her voice as she bent over to put down her glass. But Minnie did.

'I see,' said her aunt doubtfully. 'And, of course, Uncle Marty and I are delighted to have you. But— well, my dear, when I was first engaged to your uncle, two weeks apart would have seemed almost an eternity.'

'Oh, no,' said Amber, not realising that the bleakness in her voice was striking a chord of devastating pity in her aunt. 'Oh, no. Pierre and I don't feel like that at all.'

Minnie nodded, understanding that there was no more to be said. Whatever it was that was making her niece so wretchedly unhappy, it was obviously something she didn't feel able to discuss.

'I'll get you another drink,' she said, standing up because she needed something to do. 'Perhaps a little drop of something stronger in it?'

'Do I look as though I need a pick-me-up?' laughed Amber. 'Thank you, Aunt Minnie, that would be very nice.'

Yes, thought Minnie, as she took a bottle out of the sideboard. Yes, my very dear niece, you look as if you could do with a great deal more than a temporary pick-me-up. She poured a generous amount from the bottle and carried it outside to Amber who, with a faraway look in her eyes, was watching the children next door tumble, screaming, into a paddling pool which was shaped like an overfed whale.

'What are your wedding plans, dear?' asked Minnie, concluding that a discussion of practical details would be a safer topic than emotions. 'Have you and Pierre set a date?'

'Not yet. There's no particular hurry. Pierre's very busy at the moment, learning his father's business. And I'm hoping for a government job in Winnipeg, so I'd like to get settled into that before we make any plans.'

'Yes, of course.' So practical details weren't going to provide much food for conversation, either. Minnie thought back to the bright, sunny girl she had greeted at the coach depot only a year ago. Something was wrong. Very drastically wrong.

The coach depot... That young man who had drawn such sparks from Amber's eyes...

'Amber,' she said slowly, 'did you ever see any more of that attractive young coach-driver? The nice one who carried your cases?'

Amber felt colour creeping over her ears. 'The coach-driver?' she said carefully. 'What makes you ask that?'

'Well, I saw him get on the plane with you the next day. I just wondered if you'd met up with him again.'

'Yes,' said Amber briefly. 'As a matter of fact, I did.'

For the first time since her niece had arrived, Minnie saw some sign of animation, a lifting of that deadened, dreary look that was tragic in the eyes of one so young.

'Really?' she smiled. 'Did you see him in Thunder Bay, then? Is he as nice as he seemed?'

'Yes, I saw him in Thunder Bay. And yes, I suppose he is as nice as he seemed.'

He *hadn't* seemed nice, though, thought Amber. Not then. At the time, he had been thoroughly high-handed and arrogant.

The closed look descended over her face again, and a few minutes later Uncle Marty arrived home.

Amber took a long sip of lemonade, then lay back in the deck-chair and closed her eyes.

It was so peaceful out here on this sizzling summer afternoon. Peaceful in quite a different way from the peace at home. There it was all quiet, and smooth lawns, and you rarely heard children playing. Here it was warm and noisy. The children next door were splashing about in the pool and their big black dog was barking in frenzy at a cat. But it was a pleasant sort of noise. Friendly. She liked it.

The sun had continued to beat down during the entire week that she had been here, but it was cool in the house, and outside the heat was so soporific that it numbed her mind. She liked that, too.

Now Aunt Minnie had gone out to organise a church buffet supper, leaving Amber by herself to enjoy the garden and dream. Or try desperately not to dream.

A fly buzzed somewhere close to her ear and she swatted at it. A child was pushed out of the pool and screamed, as the dog made a lunge for the cat and set up a howl of protest when she swiped him with her claws. Amber sighed and opened her eyes again.

Obviously she wasn't going to sleep this afternoon, but it didn't matter, she could read instead. She took another sip of lemonade and reached out a hand for her book.

The fly buzzed her other ear and she swatted it again and turned a page. When it started exploring her nose, she swore, shook her head to dislodge it and, with a purposeful tightening of her lips, got a firm grip on the spine of her book.

'I'll fix you, you little monster,' she muttered vengefully, jumping to her feet with murder in her eye.

She could see the fly crawling over one of Aunt Minnie's plant-holders.

'Got you!' she cried, swinging the book triumphantly through the air. But she hadn't, and the fly took off, zooming above her head.

She swung round, wielding the book like a broadsword, and aimed wildly in the direction in which she thought her quarry had flown. And as her unorthodox weapon swung forward, she caught a vague glimpse of something directly in its path. Something male in a white shirt, with a golden tan—and the book was heading straight for his chest.

'Hold it, Boadicea,' said a low, warm voice she had never expected to hear again. 'I'm afraid your prey is long gone, and there's not the slightest point in your squashing me instead.'

Something burst inside Amber like a great explosion of light, and she felt a firm hand encircle her flailing wrist as the book slapped quietly down on to the wooden floor of the porch.

CHAPTER TEN

AMBER stared straight ahead of her, afraid to look up in case he wasn't real. But when she finally found the courage to raise her head he was still there, larger than life, and his eyes were even bluer than she remembered.

He was still holding fast to her wrist.

'Kyle?' she whispered, not wanting to say more in case she shattered the illusion. She still could not quite grasp that he was real.

'Yes, it's me. I don't squash easily, kitten. Although, after watching that demonstration of attempted insecticide, I think I'm rather glad I'm not a fly.'

Oh, he was real all right. He hadn't changed a bit. And he had called her kitten. The corners of her lips trembled, then widened into a long, dreamy smile.

'Toad,' she said softly. And then, as the smile grew dreamier, 'I don't want to squash you, Kyle, I want to——'

'Kiss me, I hope, kitten...' His smile, too, was very tender. 'As much as I want to kiss you.'

He was holding her wrist as if he were afraid to let her go, and now he bent her arm behind her back as his other arm came around her waist and crushed her against his chest. Then he was kissing her, and his kiss made a mockery of the lonely months without him as she returned it with all the hunger and love she had tried so hopelessly to extinguish.

Her free arm wrapped around his head, pressed his lips closer as she strained against his wonderfully long, hard body, needing to be a part of him—as she knew now she had needed almost from the moment they had met.

He gave a small, satisfied groan and his hands slid slowly up her sides until they came to rest on her shoulders. Then he held her very gently away.

'Amber,' he said, in that gloriously sensual voice which she had never for a moment forgotten. 'How I've missed you.' There was pain in the voice now, and instinctively Amber lifted her arms to give comfort. She ran soft fingers over the lines creasing his forehead, smoothing them away. And as she gazed up at him so many delicious sensations were stirring in her body that she found she could hardly think straight. Then thought wasn't necessary any more, because she knew with utter certainty that here in Kyle's arms she had come home.

But now, as the dog from next door barked again, reality began to intrude. The reality which told her that although, by some miracle, Kyle still wanted her as much as she wanted him, nothing was resolved between them. And wanting was not the same as loving.

'Kyle,' she said, her voice suddenly strained and brittle, 'what are you doing here?'

He stared at her, then shook his head as if he couldn't believe what he had heard. 'Good grief. I know you've always excelled at deflating my ego, love, but really this is going too far.' He sighed theatrically. 'Since you apparently haven't noticed, what I've been doing is kissing you. And I *thought* I was doing rather a good job.'

'You know damn well you were,' retorted Amber, trying not to laugh. 'You also know that wasn't what I meant.'

'Do I? All right. Come here, and I'll tell you whatever you want to hear.' He took a step backwards, lowered himself into the deck-chair that she had been lying in, smiled and held out his arms.

Amber stared at the lithe body in the shirt which was open almost to the waist in order to defeat the heat. Then her eyes travelled down the long legs in pale grey denim and up again to his thighs. She ran her tongue quickly over her lips and her mouth was suddenly dry.

He was gesturing at her to come closer.

Slowly, almost hypnotically, she walked towards him, and when she stood beside him he took both her hands in his and drew her down on to his lap.

'That's better,' he said. 'Now, tell me what's the matter.'

'Matter?' she exclaimed. 'You wander back into my life after ignoring me for almost ten months, and you ask *me* what's the matter.'

'OK, OK.' He was laughing at her. 'I might point out that I've also been ignored. There's no need to sharpen your claws on me, kitten.' Then, seeing her face, he sobered. 'I'm sorry. Heaven knows I don't mean to hurt you. There's been more than enough of that.'

'Yes,' said Amber, not looking at him. 'Yes, there has. Kyle . . . ?'

'Yes, love?'

'You know I told you I was going to marry Pierre?'

A shadow crossed his face, erasing the softness in his eyes. 'I'm not likely to forget,' he replied harshly.

'No. Well, you see, now—now Pierre and I are engaged. We're going to be married.'

Kyle looked up at her and there was steel in the cobalt-blue eyes. 'No,' he said emphatically, 'you're not. *That's* what I'm doing here, Amber. I came to tell you that you're not marrying anyone but me.' His hand moved possessively over her thigh, and in spite of the fact that his dictatorial tone was causing her hackles to rise as usual a different set of sensations entirely was moving her to place both arms around his neck. Besides, she needed the support, because although her heart was pumping wildly she wasn't at all sure that she believed her ears.

'What do you mean?' she asked cautiously.

'I should have thought that was obvious.'

'Kyle,' she began threateningly, 'if you don't stop this at once——'

'Stop what?' he asked, moving his hands to her shoulders and pushing purposefully at the straps of her yellow sun-dress.

Amber leaped off his lap, put her hands on her hips—and remembered just in time that she mustn't stamp her feet. 'Kyle!' she began furiously. Then the words died in her throat because all of a sudden she felt tears prick the backs of her eyes.

Kyle saw her expression change and was instantly contrite. 'Don't, Amber. I'm sorry. It's been such a long time since I had the opportunity to tease you.' He smiled, a tender, rueful smile that melted her heart. 'I couldn't resist it. Forgive me?'

He held out his arms again, and Amber looked into his eyes and saw that he, too, had suffered. His face was thinner, his cheekbones more prominent, and there were new little lines etched faintly beside his mouth. At that moment she would have forgiven him anything.

She sank down on his lap again and put her arms around him as he lifted his hand and began to weave it gently through her hair.

'I heard you were getting married,' he said quietly. 'Mother told me.'

'Yes, I wrote to her.'

'I know. I wanted to murder you the day I heard that, but I decided it just proved that I'd been right about you all along. There didn't seem much sense in going to gaol for the rather temporary pleasure of wringing your lovely neck.'

'But I was only marrying Pierre because I couldn't marry you, and because it made Father happy, and I didn't see why *somebody* shouldn't be happy...' Amber's voice rose in a despairing wail, and Kyle patted her shoulder gently.

'I know, I know. But, you see, I didn't understand that. I'd seen you kissing Pierre... All right,' he added hastily as she opened her mouth to protest. 'I'd seen *him* kissing you, and, although I'm not usually of a particularly humble disposition, it did occur, even to me, that you might find an up-and-coming young businessman a more attractive proposition than the rather ordinary driver of a coach.'

'Ordinary?' scoffed Amber. 'You? Oh, Kyle, I never did find Pierre particularly attractive. And his job doesn't matter to me any more than yours does.'

'I'm delighted to hear it,' said Kyle drily. He traced his thumb thoughtfully down the side of her face. 'Wasn't that a bit hard on Pierre, though? I mean, you were going to marry him, weren't you?'

'Oh, yes, but he doesn't think I'm all that sexy, either.'

'That was *not* the impression I had——' began Kyle disagreeably.

'I know, but that was just the mauve jumpsuit and the drink.'

'I see.' His lips quirked, and there was an odd little gleam in his eye. 'I think I have a certain sympathy for the fellow in the matter of that jumpsuit. Do you still have it?'

Amber giggled. 'I'm not going to tell you until you finish explaining what you're doing here.'

'Well, I know what I'd like to be doing.'

'Kyle——'

'All right, don't hit me.' He stopped tangling her hair and began to run his fingers up her half-bare back. 'As I said, when I heard you were going to be married I thought that was the end of that. The toad wasn't going to get the princess, so he'd better get on with his life. Oh, I did think, briefly, that I might try to do something about it. But I remembered that I *had* tried. Twice. First when I went back to your trailer after you threw me out of it—I tried to get you to eat, if memory serves—then again the next day in the shop——'

'When I told you I was going to marry a Porsche,' said Amber guiltily.

'Precisely. Oh, I heard you call after me, of course, but you were in a flaming rage, and I assumed you'd thought of a few more choice insults to hurl in my direction. Besides, I wasn't especially interested in competing with a Porsche.'

'And you never do what doesn't interest you, I suppose?'

'I do on occasions.' He smiled. 'But not with a very good grace. I may be a fool, Amber, but I don't beg. It took me a long time to realise that I loved you, and by the time I was sure you had already made your decision. Or I thought you had.' The smile broadened into a grin. 'But I forgot to make allowances for your fiery disposition—otherwise known as bad temper.'

'Toad.' Amber raised her fist and struck him squarely in the chest.

'Cat.' He caught it in his hand, pulled her on top of him and slapped her playfully on the behind.

'I think cats eat toads,' said Amber, sitting up and eyeing him reflectively.

'I wouldn't doubt it.' His eyes gleamed wickedly. 'Want to try?'

'Later,' said Amber. 'Right now we have to talk.'

Kyle sighed and stretched a long arm around her waist. 'If you say so. But it doesn't sound nearly as much fun.'

'Kyle, I'm serious.'

He nodded, his eyes suddenly grave. 'I know. Talk away, then. I'm listening.'

'You never listen.'

'I was listening that time you phoned me.' His tone was no longer teasing.

'Were you? I wondered.'

'Well, of course I was listening, you little——' He stopped and began again. 'Amber, have you any idea how I felt, hearing your voice again after all those months? For a moment I almost believed in miracles. Then you hung up on me. You *did* hang up on me, didn't you?'

Amber turned her head away and stared at a child who appeared to be climbing the fence. 'Yes, I did.'

'Why?'

'Because—because you had someone else.'

'What?'

Reluctantly Amber made herself look at him. And she saw that the blue eyes were mystified, impatient—even a little angry.

'You had someone else,' she repeated. 'There was a woman with you.'

'Someone else? Are you out of your——?' He stopped abruptly and put his hand over his eyes. 'Oh, lord. You mean Patsy Schlumberger, don't you?'

'I don't know who I mean. But she was with you, and I thought she was your girlfriend.'

'Heaven forbid.' He rolled his eyes at the sky in supplication. 'At the time, she was my friend Joe Peterson's girlfriend, but as he has a new one every week that's hardly relevant.'

Amber frowned, puzzled. 'If she was your friend's girlfriend, what was she doing in your flat?'

'She *and* Joe—not to mention Sarah and Manfred—were collecting me for a pub crawl, if I remember correctly. I don't make a point of absconding with other people's women. It's a sure way to lose good friends.'

'I didn't mean that, Kyle. I—are you telling me you weren't alone, then, with—Patsy?'

'Not unless you discount the inhibiting presence of Joe, Sarah and Manfred. Is *that* why you didn't answer when I phoned you back? I knew damn well you were there, because Mother told me you were calling from your home when I phoned her to get your number.'

'Yes.' Amber nodded sadly. 'I thought you were just being polite. I knew it was you, too.'

'I'm never polite. Hell, Amber, do you mean to tell me I've been going through hell all these months because you thought I was having an affair with Patsy Schlumberger? *Patsy Schlumberger?* You little idiot, I haven't been near another woman since I met you.

Oh, I tried, believe me, but every time I thought about taking someone else in my arms—I kept seeing your big green eyes—or are they grey?—and your adorable nose in the air, and I remembered the feel of your lovely body curved into mine . . . and I couldn't do it.'

'Oh, Kyle.' Amber bent her head and covered his face with kisses. And then Kyle pulled her into his arms and kissed her back. He kissed her neck, her hair, the hollow beneath her chin, and when he reached her mouth again and she twisted her body to get closer, the deck-chair, with a grinding squeal of protest, broke slowly apart and collapsed.

When Aunt Minnie returned home a few minutes later, and went to investigate what she regarded as very odd noises coming from the garden, all she could see at first was a tangle of arms and legs and a copper-coloured head lying very close to a blond one. The noises appeared to be howls of strangled laughter.

Aunt Minnie gave a smug little smile and stole back into the house. One dead or mutilated deck-chair was a small price to pay for the happiness of her favourite niece.

'Oh, dear,' gasped Amber, when at last their bodies were untangled and they had struggled back to their feet. 'Oh, dear. I'm afraid we owe Aunt Minnie a new chair, don't we?'

'I'm afraid we do.' Kyle draped an arm over her shoulder and surveyed the damage. 'But I don't think your commendable aunt will mind.'

'What makes you say that?'

'She came to see me at the coach depot the day before yesterday. At least, I think she came to see me—although she said she just happened to be passing.'

'What? She never ''passes'' the coach depot. What did she really want?'

'She didn't say. Just came up to me while I was loading suitcases and said she recognised me from last year. Then she happened to mention that you were staying with her—and she gave me her address.'

'Oh. Dear, wonderful, scheming Aunt Minnie!' exclaimed Amber. 'I never could hide anything from her. *Now* I understand why you came.'

'Yes, but I'd have come anyway, Amber. It would have taken longer to find you, that's all.'

Amber glanced up at him doubtfully. 'But—I thought you said you'd tried twice—three times, really, if you count phoning me back—and that you never beg.'

He shook his head, and moved his hand to the back of her neck. 'I don't. But, you see, I'd been doing some thinking. Dad was right. It was time I settled down and thought about the future. I've enjoyed my life on the roads, but now that's over. The day your aunt came was my last day on the job. I'm going back to the university, Amber. Because it's time, and because it's what I want to do.'

'As long as you're sure . . .'

'I'm quite sure. I always knew I'd go back some day, and once I'd made my decision I decided to buy a house.'

'You did?'

'Mm-hm. So I bought a big, older one not far from the university. It's a lot like this one, only larger. And it needs some work, but I quite enjoy carpentry, messing about with paint and restoring old things to their original beauty. Then I realised that the only thing missing was a wife. I thought about that some more, and finally accepted what I'd really known all along. That the only wife I wanted was you, my impossible Amber.' His hand on her neck began to massage her skin. 'I'd been a stiff-necked fool to give you up so easily. It's true that I don't beg. But I do fight for what I want. Just ask Erik.'

'I know. The doughnuts in Charmaine Oikenen's lunch-box.'

Kyle laughed. 'You remember that, do you? Well, I'd like you to know that on occasions my pugilistic instincts have had worthier motives than gluttony.'

'Such as?'

'In this case, such as winning back the woman I love from that unspeakable creature with the Porsche.'

'Pierre's not unspeakable. He's quite nice, really.'

'All right, I'll take your word for it. I can afford to be generous today. In fact, I'm sorry for the fellow. After all, he may not know it yet, but he's just lost all hope of getting you out of that mauve jumpsuit.'

Amber moved his hand off her neck and pretended to push him away. 'Is that all you ever think about?'

'Not really. I'd quite like to remove this yellow thing you're wearing, too. It doesn't look as though it would take much...' He stepped towards her, and Amber giggled and darted away.

'As a matter of fact,' she called to him from a safe distance, 'now that I think about it, I don't believe Pierre will mind really, as long as I'm the one to call it off. He was only marrying me to please his father, but I think if he has to marry anyone he'd just as soon it was little Mary Morris from his office. She's madly in love with him, and Pierre rather likes that.'

'Very natural,' said Kyle, advancing across the lawn. 'Your father won't like it, though.'

'No,' agreed Amber, backing into the fence. 'But he'll get over it. He won't have any choice.'

'Neither will you.' Kyle caught up with her and, amid howls and catcalls from the clan next door whose fence it was, he began to push at the straps which were holding up her dress.

'Kyle, stop it!' cried Amber, wriggling away from him and running towards the porch. 'You're making an exhibition of us.'

'You go ahead, miss, we don't mind,' called the eldest of the tribe next door. 'Let him take it off, then you can both have a nice, cool dip in the pool.'

'Precocious brat,' laughed Kyle, catching up with Amber and pulling her down beside him on the grass. 'I suppose I'll have to postpone that little interlude until later.'

'Much later,' said Amber primly, pulling up her straps and patting uselessly at her hair. She turned, so that she could see all of him. 'You do look—edible, Kyle, with your shirt hanging out of your jeans and all ruffled and sexy like that.'

'Ruffled and sexy? Is that what I am? Well, I suppose there are worse ways to look.'

'Definitely,' agreed Amber, as she leaned happily against his shoulder.

Kyle glanced down at the top of her head, which was shining bright copper in the sun. Then he lifted his hand and began to wind the thick tresses through his fingers.

' "Shall I compare thee to a summer's day?" ' he quoted softly.

'I shouldn't think so,' replied Amber prosaically. 'Summer days often go with rain and thunder where I come from. And I've had enough of both.'

'All right,' said Kyle, his blue eyes sparkling with mischief. 'How about this?

My mistress' eyes are nothing like the sun;
Coral is far more red than her lips' red;

If snow be white, why then her breasts are
                          dun; . . .'

'Now *wait* a minute,' protested Amber. 'There's no
need to go that far. Toad.'

'Ah,' said Kyle, 'but you forget the end, my love.

My mistress when she walks, treads on the
                          ground;
And yet, by heaven, I think my love as rare
As any she belied with false compare.'

His voice was very low, and when Amber turned
to look up at him, she saw that the cool blue eyes had
darkened to a deep and tender warmth. Suddenly she
felt a ridiculous urge to cry.

'Good old Shakespeare,' she murmured, burying
her face in his neck.

'Mmm. He rarely lets me down.' Seeing her
shoulders shake slightly, Kyle placed a finger beneath
her chin and lifted her face to his. 'What's this?' he
asked, bewildered. 'Amber, you're crying.'

There was silence for a few minutes then, as he
wiped a tear from the corner of her eye and afterwards took gentle advantage of her parted lips.

Aunt Minnie, peering through the window, nodded
with satisfaction.

Then the dog started barking at the cat again and
the lovers came down to earth.

'Dogs and kids,' muttered Kyle. 'A deadly com-
bination which inevitably results in noise.'

'Yes,' answered Amber, trailing her fingers lazily
through his hair, 'but it's a happy sort of noise, isn't
it?'

'I suppose it is,' he agreed without conviction. 'That
reminds me, did you hear that Rosie's going to add

to the population soon? She's been on a continuous shopping spree ever since she heard the news, and poor Erik can't decide if he's delighted or scared stiff.'

Amber laughed. 'He'll settle for the delight once the baby's safely born and Rosie has to stop shopping.'

'Yes, no doubt he will. *If* Rosie stops shopping.' He picked up her hand and stroked it absently. 'Do you want children, Amber?'

'Yes,' said Amber, surprising herself. 'Yes, I think I do.'

'Thank heaven.'

'Really?' Amber gaped at him. 'I didn't know you felt that strongly.'

'I don't.' He grinned. 'It's just that my father and I have been getting along rather better than usual lately. He's *almost* accepted that I have a right to run my own life. But there'd be no reasoning with him if I married a woman who didn't want to produce his grandchild.'

'So for the sake of family peace you're willing to put up with the whining and the wetting?' Amber teased him.

'Not at all. At that point I'll hand the brat over to you.'

Amber shook her head. 'Nice try,' she said sweetly. 'Think again. I'll have a job, remember?'

'In Winnipeg, I suppose,' he suggested drily. 'Leaving me in Toronto with the brat.'

'No, you idiot. Here. Where we can *share* our pride and joy.'

Kyle sighed. 'Whatever happened to the good old days?' he grumbled. 'When women looked after the children, and all men had to do was hand out cigars and brag. I think I'd do that rather well.'

'I'll bet you would. But you're not going to get the chance, because the *bad* old days died with the dodo.' She pulled a face at him. 'Are you sure you don't want to change your mind?'

'About what?'

'Me. Children——'

'No.' Suddenly Kyle was serious again. 'I'll never change my mind about you.'

She smiled up at him, wondering how she could ever have thought him cold, and at that moment he reached into his shirt pocket and pulled out a small white box. 'Close your eyes,' he ordered.

Wondering, Amber did as she was told. A moment later she felt something smooth and round slide over her ring finger.

'Now open them.'

'Oh!' she exclaimed, gazing down at the circlet of clear stones gleaming in the bright rays of the sun. 'Oh, Kyle, how beautiful! Diamonds and amethyst. It's perfect.'

Kyle, watching her radiant face, felt a surge of tenderness and passion for this contrary, exasperating, captivating woman he loved. 'I was going to give you amber and amethyst,' he told her, 'but for you only diamonds would do.'

Amber held out her hand to catch the light and said dreamily, 'What more could I possibly want?'

'Me, I hope,' Kyle mocked her gently.

'You *know* I want you.' She twisted the ring round her finger, and smiled as it sparked in the sun. 'Kyle...'

'Yes, kitten.'

'You must have been very certain . . . I mean, you had the ring, and yet the last time you saw me I told you to get out of my life. What made you so sure...?'

'I wasn't sure at all. I just hoped. And I don't know what I'd have done if my hopes had been unfounded. Probably given further thought to murder.' He smiled wryly. 'The truth is, I wasn't sure of anything until I saw your face in that timeless moment when you mistook me for a fly—and then realised it was me. I saw love in your eyes then, Amber. That was when I knew.'

'Yes,' said Amber. 'Oh, I do love you, Kyle.' Suddenly she jumped to her feet, then seized his hands to bring him up beside her. 'I love you very much.' She grinned, and batted her eyelids seductively. 'But do you love *me*? You haven't said so, you know.'

'Haven't I?' He placed his hands lightly on her shoulders and pinioned her with his eyes. 'I love you, Amber.' His voice was husky. 'More than anything in the world. I love you, and I always will.'

Their eyes locked, and for a while they were oblivious to the shouts of the children, seeing only each other. Then Kyle's expression changed and he added softly, 'That's why I decided to marry you, kitten. Because I love you.'

'Mmm,' said Amber, scuffing one sandalled toe along the grass. 'You know, I hate to mention it, Kyle, but you haven't actually asked me to marry you. You ordered me to, I think, but that's not really quite the same thing.' She lowered her lashes and fixed her eyes modestly on the ground.

'I suppose it isn't.' He sighed resignedly. 'All right, then, how's this?' Solemnly taking both her hands in his, he raised them very slowly to his lips. 'Will you marry me, Amber Jones? Before you drive me crazy?'

'Well, I don't know,' replied Amber pensively. 'The last two proposals I received came with candle-light, wine and music——'

'Too bad,' said Kyle unsympathetically. 'This time you'll have to settle for sunlight and . . .' he picked up her neglected glass and gave a grimace of distaste '. . . warm lemonade—and that awful noise from next door.'

'Oh.' Amber glanced up at him, her eyes full of mischief, then she folded her hands demurely at her waist and said with an exaggerated sigh, 'In that case, I'd better accept.'

'Yes,' said Kyle, locking her firmly in his arms. 'You'd better. And the music will come later. I promise.'

HARLEQUIN
Romance®

Coming Next Month

Available in November wherever paperback books are sold, or through Harlequin Reader Service:

In the U.S.
901 Fuhrmann Blvd.
P.O. Box 1397
Buffalo, N.Y. 14240-1397

In Canada
P.O. Box 603
Fort Erie, Ontario
L2A 5X3

Harlequin Superromance®

THEY'RE A BREED APART

The men and women of the Canadian prairies are slow to give their friendship or their love. On the prairies, such gifts can never be recalled. Friendships between families last for generations. And love, once lit, burns hot and pure and bright for a lifetime.

In honor of this special breed of men and women, Harlequin Superromance® presents:

SAGEBRUSH AND SUNSHINE
(Available in October)

and

MAGIC AND MOONBEAMS
(Available in December)

two books by Margot Dalton, featuring the Lyndons and the Burmans, prairie families joined for generations by friendship, then nearly torn apart by love.

Look for SUNSHINE in October and MOONBEAMS in December, coming to you from Harlequin.

MAG-C1R

HARLEQUIN
American Romance®

November brings you...

SENTIMENTAL
JOURNEY

BARBARA
BRETTON

Jitterbugging at the Stage Door Canteen, singing along with the Andrews Sisters, planting your Victory Garden—this was life on the home front during World War II.

Barbara Bretton captures all the glorious memories of America in the 1940's in SENTIMENTAL JOURNEY—a nostalgic Century of American Romance book and a Harlequin Award of Excellence title.

Available wherever Harlequin® books are sold.

ARSENT-1

HARLEQUIN
American Romance®

RELIVE THE MEMORIES....

From New York's Lower East Side immigrant experience to San Francisco's great quake of 1906 to the muddy trenches of World War I's western front to the speakeasies of the Roaring Twenties...A CENTURY OF AMERICAN ROMANCE takes you on a nostalgic journey through the twentieth century.

Glimpse the lives and loves of American men and women from the turn of the century to the dawn of the year 2000. Revel in the romance of a time gone by. And sneak a peek at romance in an exciting future.

Watch for all the A CENTURY OF AMERICAN ROMANCE titles coming to you one per month in Harlequin American Romance.

Don't miss a day of A CENTURY OF AMERICAN ROMANCE.

A CENTURY OF
AMERICAN ROMANCE
1940s

The women...the men...the passions...the memories....

From *New York Times* Bestselling author
Penny Jordan, a compelling novel of ruthless passion
that will mesmerize readers everywhere!

Penny Jordan

Silver

Real power, true power came from
Rothwell. And Charles vowed to have it,
the earldom and all that went with it.

Silver vowed to destroy Charles, just as surely and
uncaringly as he had destroyed her father; just as he had
intended to destroy her. She needed him to want her . . .
to desire her . . . until he'd do anything to have her.

But first she needed a tutor: a man who wanted no one.
He would help her bait the trap.

**Played out on a glittering international stage,
Silver's story leads her from the luxurious comfort of
British aristocracy into the depths of adventure,
passion and danger.**

AVAILABLE NOW!

 HARLEQUIN

SIL-1A

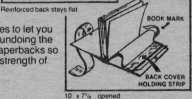